MJ

B 420

E1

£8.99

73

WOMAN OVERBOARD

Despite her misgivings about accompanying her daughter, Tamsin, on the Caribbean cruise, Kate felt excited as they boarded the ship. She had been a widow for three years and, with Tamsin's help, was now coming to terms with life without her husband, Peter. The cruise was to have been Tamsin's honeymoon, but her fiancé, Ronnie, had called off their marriage at the last minute. Both Kate and Tamsin considered themselves 'one man women', but a romantic surprise was in store for each of them.

JOY ST. CLAIR

WOMAN OVERBOARD

Complete and Unabridged

LINFORD
Leicester

First Linford Edition
published 1998

British Library CIP Data

St. Clair, Joy
    Woman overboard.—Large print ed.—
    Linford romance library
    1. Love stories
    2. Large type books
    I. Title
    823.9′14 [F]

    ISBN 0–7089–5303–4

Published by
F. A. Thorpe (Publishing) Ltd.
Anstey, Leicestershire

Set by Words & Graphics Ltd.
Anstey, Leicestershire
Printed and bound in Great Britain by
T. J. International Ltd., Padstow, Cornwall

This book is printed on acid-free paper

1

AFTER all the tensions of the past week, followed by the crowded flight to Miami and the struggle for seats on the airport bus, the arrival at the quayside had an uplifting effect on Kate. Despite her misgivings about accompanying her daughter on the Caribbean cruise, she actually sensed a surge of pleasurable anticipation.

"Must be getting skittish in my old age," she muttered, staring at the dazzling white ship lying in the morning sunshine, the top three of its seven decks liberally hung with bunting, its stately twin funnels laid back. The s.s. Jamestown Pearl.

"Oh Mum, what a magnificent sight!" exclaimed Tamsin, falling in behind her as they climbed the gangway steps to the deck. She added in a loud whisper, "I see the officers are lined up to give us the once-over." She looked to the bridge where a row of white-uniformed, gold-braided figures stood at ease, scrutinising the queue of new arrivals. "Hm! They're a handsome bunch."

Kate ran her eyes over the officers, one of whom towered above the rest and sported more gold braid. The captain, she presumed. From a distance of twenty yards she had an impression of rugged features and dark hair beneath the peaked cap.

She watched his gaze travel towards them. He gave Tamsin a cursory glance then his interest was transferred to Kate — and remained there.

Hm! Nice, she mused, if you liked big craggy types with lived-in faces. But he was wasting his time.

She was a widow just the right side of forty, well, thirty-seven to be exact. Her twenty-year-old marriage had left her with a comfortable figure and silver streaks among the blonde of her drastically short hair. Peter had been the only man she had known intimately, or ever wanted to. He had spoiled her and when he had died of a heart attack, three years ago, she'd been left helpless and unable to fend for herself. With Tamsin's help she was coming to terms with life. But she did not want another commitment.

The sudden remembrance of Peter made her shudder. What was she doing here? She couldn't go on a cruise without him. She never went anywhere without him.

Her panic began to subside. She had loved Peter but was just beginning to appreciate the single state, not to have to account to anyone for every move she made, being able to choose what she wanted to do. He hadn't been a domineering man but she had been brought up to respect a husband's wishes. Now it was quite a revelation to discover she had a mind of her own. She even surprised herself with her thoughts sometimes.

"What's the matter, Mum?" There was a tinge of concern in Tamsin's blue eyes.

Kate shook her head and waited for the panic to subside completely. "Nothing, dear." She didn't want to spoil Tamsin's holiday. "I just . . . "

"I know, you were thinking about Dad."

The captain had completed his study of Kate and moved on to the next passenger.

Kate wasn't used to being stared at by men, having Peter around had protected her from all that.

"You've made a conquest, Mum," grinned Tamsin as they waited for the chief cabin steward. "The captain, no less."

"Don't be daft!" Kate gave a snort. "He's much more interested in those young dolly birds than an old has-been like me."

Tamsin giggled. "Dolly birds? You do come out with some old-fashioned words."

4

"I am old-fashioned."

"Well we're going to change all that."

The chief cabin steward made himself known to them and checked their tickets against his clipboard. He frowned. "Oh dear, there seems to be some mistake. I have the cabin down to Mr and Mrs Ronald Kingsnorth." Then with relief, "Ah no, it's been changed to Mrs Kate Ashley and Miss Tamsin Ashley."

He waved his hand in the direction of a smart line of scarlet-jacketted stewards and one of them, a bronzed wiry man in his late thirties, stepped forward.

"This is Nelson, your cabin steward. He will see you settled and take care of you during the trip."

Nelson grinned and said, with a broad Cockney accent, "Welcome aboard the Jamestown Pearl, ladies."

"Are all the crew British?" asked Tamsin as they followed him along the passageway and down the stairs.

"Most of them, Miss. The passengers too."

"Is the captain British?" asked Kate.

"I'll say! He's from the west country, where all the best sailors come from. His ancestors served under Hood and Jellicoe."

"Really!" exclaimed Kate, impressed. Then, aware that Tamsin was watching her, she laughed self-consciously.

Their cabin was situated on Montego deck and was very comfortable with a double bed and ample room to move about.

"Only the best for Ronnie Kingsnorth," muttered Tamsin.

On the dressing table there was a pile of leaflets and the ship's daily newsapaper telling of forthcoming events.

Nelson warned them about the raised threshold and showed them how to work the radio. He opened a further door to reveal a blue-tiled bathroom suite, then with a broad wink, he went away whistling.

"He's of the opinion unattached ladies come on cruises in search of men," said Tamsin picking up a leaflet. "There are lots of goodies planned. There's a fancy-dress ball. And the captain's cocktail party. Barbecues and deck buffets, shows and all the latest films. Games and quizzes — and bingo. Oh and a 'Nostalgia Night'. They even give hints on what to wear. Tonight it's informal for dinner but tomorrow it's evening dress. Hm! I can see we're going to spend a lot of time changing." She eyed the cabin trunks, which had been deposited on the cabin floor, "I only hope we've brought enough clothes."

Tamsin sat gingerly on the bed. "It's going to seem funny sleeping in the bed I should have shared with Ronnie . . ." She broke off as a sob caught in her throat.

"Tamsin, love." Kate put an arm round her daughter's trembling shoulders. "You've been very brave, but I know how upset you are. After all,

7

this was to have been your honeymoon cruise."

Tamsin blinked defiantly. "I'm not upset. And Ronnie needn't think I'm going to sit at home and mope. It'll take more than a jilting to get me down."

Kate's expression softened. Ronnie Kingsnorth was an accountant in Maidstone. When Tamsin landed the job as his personal assistant it had been love at first sight. But with the wedding a week away, Ronnie had 'done a bunk'. Phoning from Scotland he said there wasn't going to be any wedding. He wasn't sure enough, he wasn't ready enough, he wasn't old enough.

Tamsin was heartbroken and Kate had the task of telling everybody the wedding was off.

The honeymoon cruise had already been booked and paid for and the girls at the office persuaded Tamsin to go on the cruise alone. And she in turn had persuaded Kate to accompany her.

Kate had never been further than the Isle of Wight. Peter wasn't one for adventure. He worked hard in an insurance office and liked somewhere where he could relax by day and go for a nice walk in the evening. But Tamsin had been determined to go, with or without Kate. Although she was a vivacious nineteen-year-old with a friendly disposition, she would need a companion to get her through this bad patch. So Kate arranged to take time off from her part-time job and they had told the travel-agents about the change of passengers.

Kate had not worked during her marriage, there had been no need. Peter earned a good salary and he preferred her to be at home looking after the house and their daughter. Kate considered herself lucky. But when he died she realised she wasn't cut out for anything. She had been good at maths at school and when the local supermarket advertised for mature women to work on the checkouts she applied for and got the job.

Tamsin pushed her fingers through her thick haze of golden hair. "I'm not going to pine. I'm going to enjoy myself. I might even leave the ship married."

Kate grinned. "Marriage on the rebound would not be a good idea."

"Perhaps not. The trouble is I'm a one-man woman." Tamsin studied her reflection in the dressing table mirror and dabbed a tissue to the corners of her china-blue eyes. "Nothing to stop you having a good time though." She turned suddenly and said in an excited tone, "Perhaps you'll go home married."

"And pigs might fly," countered Kate. "I'm a one-man-woman too."

"Yeah, sorry." Tamsin sat in an armchair, content to watch her mother unpack. "But you ought to try to find someone else. Dad wouldn't have wanted you to be lonely."

"I'm not lonely. I've got you and my job and my friends." Kate carried a pile of clothes across to the wardrobe. "I couldn't go through all that dating business again. Don't you worry about me. You're the one who's got to get up, dust yourself off and start all over again."

"You know?" Tamsin's voice grew wistful. "I can't bring myself to hate Ronnie. If he walked in right now I reckon I'd forgive him."

They finished the unpacking and went outside to watch the ship sail. A military band on the dock played marching songs and sea shanties and everyone lined the rails to throw streamers ashore. As the great ship slid majestically from its mooring, Kate glanced towards the bridge and imagined the activity taking place there. She could see white-uniformed figures moving about beyond the windows and found herself straining her eyes to pick out one who was taller than the rest. It wasn't like her at all, she mused idly. But she had to admit the sailing had been accomplished with precision.

There were electronic charts in the foyer which gave information about the ship's progress. By pressing various buttons they discovered the distance to the first port-of-call — 800 miles to Cozumel, the present average speed of the ship — 18.93 knots, and weather news — fine and clear today with a risk of heavy rain in the early hours of the following morning, soon clearing.

"Hey! There's information about the crew too!" exclaimed Tamsin excitedly. "The captain's name is Damon Penrose and he's been in charge of this vessel for three years. It doesn't give his age or marital state, unfortunately, but I'd say he's forty-fivish, wouldn't you?"

"With a wife in every port," finished Kate. "I wish you'd stop your teasing. You know very well the captain isn't interested in me."

"He could be . . . "

"Really. We exchanged one glance."

"Sometimes one glance is enough."

"It was long enough for him to see I'm a dreary housewife who's quite definitely past it."

"Never!" Tamsin changed the subject. "Come on, let's explore."

They discovered dance floors, night-clubs, a cinema, a supermarket, a boutique and a trendy gift shop selling expensive trinkets and refrigerated orchids.

Back in the cabin Kate held up a pink halter top and grey shorts. "Do you think I should? With all this cellulite?"

"Live dangerously," was Tamsin's reply. "And what cellulite?"

Kate ventured outside to settle beside one of the pools while Tamsin set off to walk the other decks.

It was July and would have been too hot but for the pleasant breeze. Kate covered her head with a floppy sunhat and donned a pair of sunglasses to protect her eyes from the glare of the sparkling deep-blue sea.

They sailed through the Straits of Florida between the coasts of America and Cuba without being able to see either shore. Kate listened to the happy cries of the people in the pool and had almost dropped off to sleep when she heard Tamsin addressing her.

"I've been checking on our fellow passengers. Most of them are married couples. There only seem to be a hundred young people and the fellas are outnumbered by the girls by two to one." Tamsin's eyes twinkled. "But I expect the crew help to redress the balance."

Kate shielded her eyes. "I expect so."

"Talking of crew, there's the captain walking on the bridge. Obviously come out to take a closer look at you."

Kate watched him pace about. Even at this distance there was no denying he was a fine figure of a man, maybe half a stone overweight, but on him it looked good. It always did on a man. There was an animal keenness about his tense stride as if the uniform he wore barely held his vitality in check. Oo-er! thought Kate, amazed by her thoughts.

"We're too far away for him to see us clearly."

"Not so," said Tamsin, "He's got binoculars. And they're trained this way!"

Kate turned her head and caught the flash of sunlight on glass. "I doubt if it's me he's watching. More like that woman over there." And she inclined her head towards a ravishing redhead lying close by.

The first sitting for lunch was announced over the loudspeakers and they went one deck down to the Fiesta dining-room where a buffet table was laid out with a mouthwaterng display of savouries and cream-covered desserts.

"I'm going to put on pounds," grumbled Kate. "I'm overweight as it is."

In the late afternoon the chief officer, standing on the bridge platform, directed lifeboat drill through a loudhailer.

"Ladies and gentlemen, we have eight hundred passengers and five hundred crew. Each lifeboat holds a hundred persons and there are thirteen lifeboats. So it works out just right."

A ripple of conversation went through the assembled passengers.

"Added to which we have two-hundred launchable liferafts and three percent of our deck material is buoyant in accordance with the law."

Kate and Tamsin were in lifeboat number ten which was in the charge of a junior officer who was wearing a lifejacket. He was an athletic-looking young man with an engaging habit of flicking his fingers through his luxuriant mane of bronze hair.

"He's handsome!" breathed Tamsin.

"And knows it!"

He informed the high-spirited crowd surging about him that he was 'Sparks' Ingram, the radio officer, and asked for a volunteer.

Kate had read that they always picked a pretty girl to demonstrate the correct way to wear a lifejacket and she wasn't surprised when he beckoned Tamsin to come forward.

She did so to a round of applause.

He gave her an intimate smile and placed the orange-coloured lifejacket over her head, but she was a very well-developed girl and he was soon all fingers and thumbs.

"You're tickling," she said, as they collapsed with laughter.

"Which boat does the captain go in?" Kate asked.

"Oh, he goes down with the ship," said Sparks blithely.

They completed the drill and Kate returned to the cabin to take a shower. She had donned her robe and was staring out of the wide window when Tamsin burst in bubbling with excitement.

"Guess what! Sparks has invited us to the officers' cocktail party in the messroom at seven."

"Us?" Kate raised her brows.

"I told him I'd only come if you were invited too."

"Thanks. I am capable of making my own arrangements."

"Are you?" Tamsin kicked off her sandals. "Mum, this is a special party for the select few. The captain may be there."

"With his own guests."

"Oh, stop making excuses," said Tamsin, wriggling out of her shorts. "I'm taking you in hand, as of now."

"What if I don't want to go?"

"Then I shan't go," she said stubbornly. "I mean it."

"Very well." Kate gave an exaggerated sigh. "I know when I'm beaten."

Kate dressed carefully in a calf-long dress of turquoise satin. It was quite plain apart from the silver belt and she wondered if it was fashionable enough. She wasn't one for dressing up. Peter had liked her in simple things and they hadn't socialised much. Her hair was really faded now although it had once been as golden as Tamsin's. She had never considered herself beautiful and Peter had never said she was, but she

18

couldn't be too bad because people said Tamsin took after her. And Tamsin *was* beautiful.

"You look really lovely, Mum." Tamsin pulled on a yellow dress with a low scooped neckline and very full skirt. There came a knock on the door and she crossed the cabin towards it. "That'll be our . . . my escort."

Kate watched Tamsin suspiciously. "What are you up to?"

"Now don't be cross. Sparks is bringing someone for you."

Kate's heart sank. Even in her teens she had dreaded the blind date. She wasn't ready for it now and her panic was very real. "Oh Tamsin, I can't . . . "

"Too late." Tamsin threw open the door. "Hi!" she greeted the two uniformed figures. They each had their caps tucked under their arms and their lapels bore the logo of the company — a dolphin on a wave.

"You look terrific, Tamsin," said Sparks as he stepped over the threshold.

He turned to introduce the good-looking man accompanying him. "This is the ship's doctor, Guy Lewis."

Kate studied the lean-limbed doctor. Goodness! she thought, he's ten years younger than me!

He had a baby-soft face, dark red hair and the friendliest hazel eyes she had ever encountered. They were returning her scrutiny with frank interest. "Kate Ashley?" He lifted her hand to his lips. "Enchanted!"

"How do you do?" she murmured.

Sparks added, "Oh yes, and he's a regular ladies man."

"So I see," said Kate, picking up her bag and shawl. At once the doctor took the latter and draped it about her shoulders.

The officers' messroom was crammed with people all talking at once. Kate quickly ascertained the captain wasn't there and felt the knot of nervous tension unravel in her stomach. How ridiculous she was being! As if it mattered who was there.

Sparks and Guy each grabbed a couple of glasses of white wine from a passing tray.

"Cheers, Kate!" said Guy placing one in her hand.

Kate clinked her glass against his and willed her nerves to grow calm. Heavens! It was only an twelve-day cruise. She wasn't likely to meet any of these people again, so why not try to relax. Besides Guy seemed quite pleasant.

They laughed and talked, shouting to be heard above the din, and Kate learned that Guy was a fully qualified surgeon and physician who had served on the s.s. Jamestown Pearl for the past three years.

"You'll be able to go ashore on five islands," he told her. "Cozumel, Jamaica, Great Inagua, San Salute and Cat Island. I'd like to escort you on a couple of them, if I can get the time off."

"Why?" Kate asked quite innocently.

"Because . . . " He looked baffled

and scratched his head. "I'm afraid I'll have to have notice of that question."

Tamsin dug Kate in the ribs and hissed, "Say yes, you twit!"

"And I'll escort you, Tamsin," said Sparks eagerly, slicing his hand through his bronze thatch.

It was some twenty minutes later when Kate was running out of small talk that she noticed the door open to admit the captain. Hers was not the only female head that swivelled in his direction, a fact that was not lost on Guy.

"Yeah, a captain's always a romantic figure, just by virtue of being a captain," he observed, "Women can't help but fall. He's a prize catch."

"Married?" asked Tamsin with a sly grin in Kate's direction.

"No, he's a widower, has been for years," replied Guy. "He was very young when he married. But I warn you, now he doesn't believe in sailors marrying. However he's that dangerous age when men on their own start

22

worrying about what they might be missing. Frankly I didn't expect to see him here tonight. He doesn't usually grace us with his company the first night out. Too much of a workaholic."

"All work and no play," said Sparks, winking at Tamsin.

Kate saw the captain's eyes scan the gathering in that same thorough manner with which he had inspected the new arrivals and she quickly looked away before they reached her. She watched him instead in the mirror behind the bar. He wore a short black cut-away jacket and there was a distinctive air of authority about him. Without his cap she saw that his hair, thick and dark short by modern standards — though not as short as her own — sprang vigorously from a straight hairline.

He could hardly be called handsome. His features were far too rugged for that — dark imposing brows, gaunt cheeks, sharp aquiline nose, firm unyielding mouth and granite chin. Put together they indicated a wealth of experience and formed a most interesting whole which elicited in Kate a desire to know more about him.

She was startled to see him watching her reflection and quickly harnessed her wayward thoughts. For a moment she held his gaze before he was forced to look away as the bosomy redhead they had seen that morning addressed him.

Kate saw Tamsin whisper something in Sparks' ear and the young man grinned. "So you want to meet the captain, do you, Kate? Guy's the man to arrange that. They're buddies."

Kate darted Tamsin a withering glance.

"I don't see why I should introduce you," said Guy. "I would be doing myself a disservice."

"Please don't bother," Kate said, "Tamsin didn't mean it."

It was too late. The captain had moved to the centre of the room and Guy was already speaking to him.

"Damon, may I present Mrs Kate Ashley and Miss Tamsin Ashley." He paused. "Ladies, Captain Penrose."

Kate, taller than average, was used to conversing with men eye-to-eye, but she had to look up to Captain Penrose. Too much of this and she could get a crick in her neck, she mused. She wondered idly how he fitted into the regulation bunk and whether he had to duck when inspecting the engine room.

They shook hands all round and Kate was disturbed by the tingle of excitement which shot up her arm from the captain's firm grip. It was like being plugged into a power point. What ever was the matter with her? She couldn't remember when she had last reacted to a man's touch so positively and she put it down to the wine, the uniform, even the unfamiliar shipboard atmosphere . . .

She returned his easy smile and noticed there were streaks of silver in his dark hair. His green eyes were densely fringed with black lashes, true seafarer's eyes, their shade and depth changing with the ebb and flow of his thoughts. They were calm now, but held a hint of a tempest ready to blow up at any time. Kate didn't think she'd like to be around when that happened. Intrigued, she was surprised to detect an underlying sadness in his expression, a slight wry twist to the mouth which gave him an unexpected air of vulnerability.

"How do you do?" His voice was deep and he spoke very correctly with the accent of an 'officer and a gentleman'.

He bent towards her. "I didn't catch your title. Is it Mrs or Miss?"

A devil raised its head in Kate's unconsciousness as she strove to gather her wits about her. She had never felt so out of her depth in her life. "Ms."

"Ms." He repeated it with an exaggerated buzz. "It's unpronounceable. Is it absolutely necessary?"

Oh dear, thought Kate, wishing she'd never started this. Well, she'd gone too far now to back down. She rifled her brain for an answer. "When a man asks a woman Mrs or Miss he's asking if she's married or not. A woman would not be expected to ask such a question of a man." She couldn't believe she'd said that and felt Tamsin's arm dig her in the ribs.

He looked as if he didn't know what had hit him. Poor man. After all he had only asked an innocent question. Kate waited to see how he would react.

"Are you asking if I'm married, Ms Ashley?" he neatly turned the tables. "The answer is no."

Kate was aware of a warm glow creeping up from her throat to infuse her cheeks. She felt awful and her one thought was to get away from there before she made any more stupid remarks.

He observed her heightened colour and smiled broadly, displaying teeth that were strong and white but a little too crooked to be false.

"Stop it, you two," said Tamsin impatiently. "Kate is my mother and she's Mrs. She's a widow."

The captain sipped from his glass and studied Kate over the rim. "We can get over the problem by using first names . . . Kate," he said at last.

"Yes, Damon."

"Excuse me, Captain . . . "

Several people, mostly women, were still waiting to speak to him and he made his apologies before turning away. Kate watched them using their body language to signal their interest, and marvelled at the boldness of her own sex.

The guests were drifting away to dinner and she allowed Guy to steer her outside.

"Well, you messed that up," whispered Tamsin as they were crushed together in the lift. "Why weren't you nice to Damon? I despair of you sometimes." She giggled suddenly. "Guy's okay though, isn't he?"

"Apart from the fact that I'm old enough to be his mother."

"Oh, there you go, on about age

again. I'm not asking you to marry him. This is a twelve-day cruise, remember. We shan't see them again. Just be nice." She added, "And you're not old enough to be his mother."

"As good as."

"He's probably older than he looks, those baby-faced men usually are."

Kate glanced warily across the lift and met Guy's laughing hazel eyes over the sea of heads between them. He winked.

"There!" murmured Tamsin. "He's quite smitten with you."

★ ★ ★

The seating arrangements for dinner were formal and permanent for the duration of the voyage, unless of course one was invited to dine with the captain. Each of the circular tables seated twelve and was presided over by one of the officers and Kate was amazed to find she and Tamsin had been allotted to Guy's table.

"No, it wasn't luck," he confessed. "I had to bully the chief table steward. He wasn't at all pleased having to alter his table plan at this late hour. Sparks wasn't pleased either but I outrank him and I figured you and your daughter would want to sit at the same table."

Throughout the lavish seven courses the doctor regaled his table guests with amusing tales of surgical operations at sea.

The captain's table was right next to theirs and though Kate sat with her back to Damon, she was conscious of him the whole time. He was obviously keeping his table amused for great gusts of laughter rose from them at regular intervals. A couple of times she was compelled to look over her shoulder at him and was chagrined each time when he met her gaze, a little smile twisting the corner of his mouth. She was determined to ignore him but he wasn't a man to be easily ignored and her eyes continued to stray in his direction, almost of their own volition.

Directly the meal finished she saw him rise and make for the door.

"Where's the captain off to?" asked Tamsin.

"Gone to get his head down for a couple of hours, I expect," said Guy. "He's taking the middle watch later."

Kate arched her brows. "Surely the captain isn't expected to take his turn on watch!"

"The captain's on duty twenty-four hours a day," said Guy. "He doesn't have to, but he likes to take the middle watch."

"What's the middle watch?"

"Midnight till four in the morning. Deadly!"

Kate accompanied Guy down the stairs to the Jolly Jack Tar Disco, wondering if she would be able to keep up with all the young ones crowding in there. It had been a long day.

"I'd rather sit out on the deck," she said. "You don't have to come too. Stay and dance with the young girls."

He didn't take the lifeline she offered

him. Instead he slipped a protective arm around her shoulders and said, "Out on deck will be fine."

They leaned against the rail and stared out over the moonlit sea, so still and calm the ship hardly appeared to be moving.

"The water looks like silk," said Kate. "It's so quiet it's almost eerie."

"A painted ship on a painted ocean," quoted Guy.

He turned her to face him and transferred his hands to her shoulders. The skeins of tinted lights overhead were muted but it was easy to see the glitter in his hazel eyes. She had not reached the ripe old age of thirty-seven without knowing when a man was about to kiss her even though in her case it was usually a colleague of Peter's at the staff Christmas party.

As Guy's lips swooped towards her she turned her head and received his kiss on her cheek.

"Kate," he whispered, "Don't be coy." He captured her face in his hands and brought his lips deliberately to hers.

Her only reaction was to pull away. "I'm sorry, Guy, it's not you. It's just . . ." She struggled for words to let him down lightly. "You're going too fast for me."

"Ah, when eternity is twelve days it's a crime to waste one minute."

It sounded like a well worn line and it was a relief to laugh.

There came a familiar crackle over the loudspeakers then the words, "Will Doctor Lewis contact the sick-bay please."

"Damn!" Guy walked to the telephone on the wall while Kate glanced idly about her.

All at once she saw the captain bearing down on her, cap in hand.

He nodded to her cordially then cocked an inquisitive eyebrow at Guy as he replaced the receiver.

"Suspected coronary." Guy planted a swift kiss on Kate's startled mouth. "There'll be other nights, my dear," he promised before striding away.

For long moments Kate and the captain stared at each other and she was unnerved to experience a flutter in the region of her stomach. She didn't like the way her body was responding to him and was angry with herself for allowing him to affect her in this way — and for allowing it to matter.

At last he spoke. "I see you're getting into the shipboard routine of moonlight and romance."

"When eternity is twelve days it's a crime to waste one minute," she countered.

He laughed. "I couldn't have put it better myself." He turned to rest his elbows on the rail. "You're hard to fathom."

"You've only known me five minutes."

"I'm a great believer in first impressions."

"So am I."

He was standing so close she could detect the tang of his aftershave, spicy with a hint of sandalwood.

Eight bells sounded nearby, proclaiming the start of the middle watch. The captain straightened and stared at Kate in a frankly appraising way.

Taking little gulps of air, acutely conscious of her quickening pulses, she gazed up at him with alarm. Was he going to kiss her? Oh she hoped not. She couldn't handle it.

"Don't look at me like that, Kate," he said with a chuckle. "As if I'm the big bad wolf and you're Little Red Riding Hood. I'm not going to eat you."

She realised then he was teasing her and laughed with relief.

He placed his cap on his head and saluted smartly. "Goodnight, Kate, sweet dreams."

She went to her cabin to prepare for bed, still disconcerted by her mind's preoccupation with Damon Penrose. Never had her thoughts been so wrapped around a perfect stranger.

As she climbed into bed she heard

Tamsin bid someone goodnight outside the door.

She came in yawning.

"Was that Sparks?"

"Yes. He's a real charmer."

"Did he tell you that when eternity is twelve days it's a crime to waste one minute?"

"Something like that." Tears welled up in Tamsin's eyes.

At once Kate was out of bed and cuddling her daughter. "Oh dear, what's the matter, Tammy? Was it Sparks? Did he come on too strong?"

"No, he was as good as gold. Under different circumstances I could easily have fallen for him." She turned and threw herself on the bed. "He must have found me poor company. I just can't help remembering this was supposed to be my honeymoon cruise." And she wept as if her heart was breaking.

2

THEY awoke to the sound of torrential rain lashing the window.

"Look at it!" wailed Tamsin. "We might as well have stayed at home."

"I expect it's one of those tropical storms the brochure warned us about," murmured Kate. "They soon blow over."

Nelson confirmed Kate's optimistic outlook when he breezed in with the coffee and news-sheets.

"The forecast is clear skies by mid-morning, so you'll be able to go on deck and enjoy yourselves." His eyes twinkled. "I trust you had a good time yesterday?"

"We certainly did." Tamsin looked at Kate and grinned slyly. "Nelson, what do the crew think of the captain?"

"They respect him," he replied

proudly. "A sailor always admires a courageous skipper."

"Courageous?" asked Kate. "I shouldn't have thought there's much call for courage on a cruise ship."

"That's where you're wrong, Madam." Nelson sounded offended. "Life at sea is never routine. It helps to know the skipper's got what it takes. Sometimes we have to give aid to vessels in distress. Only last year Captain Penrose was awarded a medal for his part in rescuing survivors from a merchantman in trouble in rough seas."

Tamsin said: "Last night someone mentioned the captain disapproves of sailors marrying. Are you married, Nelson?

"I'll say! I've got five kids!" He delved into an inside pocket and produced some snaps.

Kate took them and made the necessary remarks of approval then passed them to Tamsin. "I don't think I'd like to be married to a sailor. Don't you miss your wife?"

"Of course. But we make up for it when I get home."

The breakfast room was practically deserted when they arrived for the sea had turned choppy and most of the passengers had decided to skip breakfast.

"We must be good sailors," said Tamsin, tucking into bacon and eggs. "Ronnie said I'd be as sick as a dog . . . " She broke off. "Help! Why do I keep thinking of that rat Ronnie?"

"You can't be expected to forget him in a couple of days."

"I suppose not." Tamsin sighed deeply. "How can you love a guy who treats you like dirt?" She pushed her plate away and stood up. "I'm going to take a walk round the deck. They say five times round is a mile." She gathered together her bag, sunglasses and paperback. "I'll see you later by the pool."

Kate was draining her coffee-cup when a shadow fell over the table.

"There you are!" said Guy Lewis, sliding his long legs under the table to sit in the chair vacated by Tamsin. "I see the rough weather didn't impair your appetite."

She grinned. "Have you eaten?"

"Yes, hours ago." He transfixed her with an intimate smile. "Sorry I had to break up the party last night."

"How's your patient?" she asked quickly.

"The coronary? It turned out to be indigestion." He shot her a cheeky glance. "The promising evenings I've had ruined by over-indulgence."

She laughed out loud. "How many trips do you make in a year?"

"Twenty-four."

"Are you continually touring the Caribbean?"

"No, we have three cruise routes." He helped himself to coffee. "Panama and Mexico besides this and they vary from seven to twenty-one days. Join the merchant navy and see the world."

"What about leave?"

"We take five days off between cruises and the ship becomes a dockland restaurant and hotel during that time. Very popular and booked up months ahead. Then we get regular leave when we return home — in my case to Yorkshire."

"Not much fun for the wives."

"No, Damon's got a point there."

"And yet he was once married himself?"

"Ah, yes. Rather intriguing. He doesn't talk about it."

"I see," she said slowly. Something must have happened that would account for the air of sadness she had sensed about him.

Guy glanced at a huge chronometer on his wrist. "I start morning surgery in ten minutes, but I'll be at your service later."

"I think I should warn you." Kate self-consciously twisted her table napkin into a tight ball. "I'm not looking for romance. Tamsin's been through a bad patch and I'm here to hold her hand. I'd hate you to waste your time on me."

"Don't you worry about my time. And don't be sure you're not looking for romance. I've already marked you down as different from the usual batch of unattached. So has the Skipper, I reckon."

She stared in surprise. "Have you been discussing me?"

"I joined him on the bridge last night." Guy paused. "If you want to know what men discuss in the deadly hours, I can tell you. Women!"

Guess what women discuss, thought Kate.

"I'm surprised," went on Guy. "He's not usually interested in the female passengers." He stood up. "Well, I'll see you later."

Oh dear! she thought watching him weave among the tables. It appeared she hadn't got through to him about not wanting romance. And Tamsin was still pining for Ronnie. She wondered if they had done right in coming on the cruise. All at once twelve days did in fact seem an eternity. How were they going to get through it, without sustaining inconsolable emotional injuries?

* * *

Kate spent most of the morning in the pool then took coffee with Mr and Mrs Young, an elderly couple from Cornwall who had been at the same dinner table the previous evening.

Just before lunch Tamsin put in an appearance with a dark-haired Adonis in tow. "Mum, this is Harry Brown. He's an Australian and a graduate from Sydney university. He's just been jilted too so we've been commiserating with each other."

Harry nodded to Kate and cast an admiring glance in Tamsin's direction, plainly bowled over.

The three of them lunched together then joined a group of people for a guided tour of the ship.

First stop was the engine room and

Kate was fascinated by all the modern equipment in use. She knew the days of coal fuel and black-faced stokers were long since past but even so was taken aback by the press-button efficiency and spotless white overalls of the crew. She thought wistfully of her father who had been an engineer. How he would have appreciated this engine room.

They found Sparks Ingram on duty in the radio-room, in charge of half a dozen operators. He appeared surprised and not a little aggrieved to see Tamsin and Harry together and he fixed them with a sullen glare. He then proceeded to throw his weight, dragging Tamsin across the room to point out various instruments and completely ignoring Harry's questions.

"What's eating that guy?" asked Harry as they prepared to leave. "Do you and he have a special understanding?"

"I wouldn't say that," she replied uneasily, obviously disturbed by the tension generated by the two men.

"I saw you dancing with him last night." Harry stared over his shoulder and glowered at Sparks. "It looked very cosy. I guess he considers you his private property."

"Don't be silly!" Tamsin blushed furiously. "I'm not anybody's private property."

"I hope Harry and Sparks aren't going to fight over you," whispered Kate in the passageway.

The party moved to the bridge and Kate was annoyed to feel her heartbeat quicken at the prospect of meeting Damon again. It wasn't likely he would show them over the place personally but it was feasible to suppose he would be around somewhere. Wasn't it?

The chief officer was waiting to greet them and Damon lurked in the background, leaning against an instrument panel. He straightened at the sight of Kate and allowed his eyes to trail over her cheesecloth shirt, brief shorts and long bare legs. She met his gaze challengingly, wishing she could overlook the delicious shiver that slithered notch by notch down her spine.

Their eyes remained locked for long moments then Damon turned away to address the chief officer who had just started to speak. "Okay Mr Burke, I'll take over."

The man looked surprised but said nothing.

"Welcome to the s.s. Jamestown Pearl, ladies and gentlemen," began Damon. "The ship is a twin-screw passenger vessel with two J. Brown steam turbine engines. We have a top speed of twenty-two knots and our horsepower is twenty-four thousand." He pointed out the modern equipment for navigation and safety and explained how the various fire alarms worked, managing to sound as if he had not said it all countless times before.

Kate was surprised by the vastness of the bridge — for it was the width of the ship — and once again impressed by the quiet efficiency of the seamen on watch.

"Any questions?" asked Damon some fifteen minutes later.

The passengers looked non-plussed and there was an awkward silence as they racked their brains for inspiration.

"How about you, Kate?" he invited her cordially.

Kate always felt sorry for speakers at this stage although she had never asked questions for fear of getting the wrong end of the stick and embarrassing Peter. She glanced down at the brief notes they had been handed as they had entered the bridge. It listed all the details of the ship. She ran her eyes quickly over it and leapt in with: "What's your fuel oil capacity?"

There, that should give him something to think about, she thought gleefully. He wouldn't be expecting an intelligent question from her, rather a query about who made the cabin curtains.

He took it in his stride. "Four-thousand long tons."

She squinted surreptitously at the paper in her hand. Dare she go on? "And diesel?"

"Seventy-eight."

"Fresh water?"

"One-thousand, two-hundred."

"What's your draught?"

"Twenty-nine feet."

She'd better stop now. She was bound to get in trouble if she continued. The questions and answers had bounced back and forth like a tennis ball and everyone had paused to listen, including the crew.

Kate had enjoyed the discourse and felt sure Damon had too.

"Is that it?" he enquired.

Just one more. "What is the moulded breadth of the ship?"

But it proved to be her undoing for a sultry-voiced woman called from the back of the group, "More important, what is the moulded breadth of the captain?"

Everyone laughed and the questioning came to an end. Kate saw it was the glamorous redhead who had deflated her.

"Bad luck, Mum," said Tamsin. "You were doing so well, before that woman upstaged you."

"Serves me right for showing off."

"Where did you learn all that stuff?"

"I cheated. I read it off the leaflet."

"Well, you certainly fooled everyone, including me."

They bid a temporary farewell to Harry and went to their cabin to change for the captain's welcoming cocktail party.

Standing in the entrance foyer to the Windsor Lounge Damon had a handshake and a smile for everyone as they filed past after giving their name to the officer on duty. At ten a minute it took well over an hour and Kate admired his stamina.

She was one of the last to greet him and was amazed that he still had the strength to grasp her hand so firmly.

"You look very nice in that get-up, Kate." He grinned wearily, taking in her lilac evening pants suit, purple blouse and gold matchstick earrings. She had been reluctant to buy the outfit but Tamsin had said all her clothes were oldfashioned. She had been sure she would never have the courage to wear it. To her eyes the colours clashed but Tamsin insisted those old rules no longer applied. She couldn't imagine what had prompted her to put it on this evening.

"Thank you," she murmured.

"Did you get all the information you wanted this afternoon?"

"Yes, thank you."

"It was very stimulating. I enjoyed it."

"So did I." Kate allowed herself a wry smile. "I was flying high for a while until I got shot down in flames."

"How come you know all those technical terms?"

"Er . . . " Should she own up? "My father was an engineer and sometimes I thought I'd like to be one." At least that was true.

"What stopped you?"

"Oh, I don't know. I got married . . . "

"And he didn't want a working wife, I suppose."

"No, it wasn't like that . . . " She stopped. It was exactly like that. Why had she never admitted it even to herself before?

She felt a hot flush of shame. For the first time in her life she had harboured a disloyal thought towards Peter's memory.

"Well, I think you would have made a good engineer."

She freed her hand at last. "Don't patronize me."

"No, I mean it. You're a clever girl."

"Oh, captain, shut up!"

"I thought we agreed to use first names . . . Kate."

"Yes, we did."

He was waiting.

"Damon."

* * *

After dinner Tamsin went off to the disco and Kate was perturbed to see both Sparks and Harry follow the girl out of the dining-room.

Guy escorted Kate down to the Mainbrace Lounge where modern ballroom dancing was in progress. She discovered he was an accomplished, predictable dancer and she only had to keep in step. This gave her a chance to look about her. She saw Damon enter and immediately invite someone to dance.

"Poor sap!" Guy followed Kate's gaze. "He's expected to spread himself around on captain's night. Not like me. I can dance the night away with the woman of my choice."

"But why me?" She was genuinely puzzled. What could a personable young man like Guy see in her? She was too old for him. She wasn't used to late nights and would be yawning soon. There were so many young and pretty girls on board and she felt a fraud for monopolising him.

"Why not?"

He was most attentive, making sure he had every dance with her, jumping to his feet and propelling her onto the floor whenever he saw someone else approaching.

She guessed it must be part of the softening up process. He would expect her to go to his cabin later. The thought filled her with dismay. Apart from not knowing how to handle such a situation, she was ashamed of her body. She had a spare tyre and the start of a varicose vein. Besides she just wasn't that kind of person. She had only known one man intimately and didn't want anyone else. Anyway she thought sex was overrated. It was exciting to begin with but then it became a habit. Oh God! she thought, how will I get rid of him?

Later, when Guy was at the bar getting more drinks, Damon asked her to dance.

Ignoring warning bells ringing in her head, she rose and went into his arms.

The band was playing a tango and she wished it were a simpler dance. She had no wish to make a fool of herself even though he was dancing with her as part of his duty. Peter had not been over fond of dancing but he had learned as it would be useful in his job when he attended social gatherings and would be called on to dance with the president's wife. So she was a bit rusty.

He was an excellent dancer and she wondered if it was part of an officer's training. He proceeded to show off, in the nicest possible way, twirling her about him and tossing her from arm to arm in such a masterly manner she couldn't have put a foot wrong if she'd tried. She was exhilarated by the way he sent her spinning away from her only to reverse the process with a light jerk of his hand which brought her back into his arms.

"Stop!" she gasped. "I shall fall over."

He gave her a final dip and led her back to her table where she flopped down, exhausted.

Guy, cradling a glass in his hand, looked peeved.

Damon did a half bow to him. "One partner returned."

"There was no need for you to dance with Kate," he grumbled. "Your brief is to dance with the unattatched."

"Sorry, I didn't know she was with you."

"Oh really?"

They stared, vaguely annoyed, at each other and Kate was upset. She couldn't allow two men to argue over her. It was just too bizarre for words. "Is that my drink?" she asked Guy, picking up the glass on the table and turning to Damon. "Thank you for the dance, captain."

She saw the tension remain in their expressions and it made her nervous. She had never experienced anything like this before and didn't know what to do or say. At the back of her mind was the thought that she had led a sheltered life.

She picked up her bag and shawl and said: "Well, I'm going to freshen up."

Guy half rose from his chair and Damon stepped aside.

She walked briskly to the ladies room but before she got there she stopped and looked round. Neither man was watching her so she quickened her step and went out of the Mainbrace Lounge by the nearest exit door.

She was in a little area filled with fruit machines. The place was crowded with people trying their luck. She went to the counter and changed a five-pound note into twenty-pence pieces then waited till a machine became free. Presently she perched on a stool clutching her plastic cup of coins and concentrated on what she was doing.

She was successful for a while and the money in her cup reached the rim but she risked it all and finally lost it. It was no surprise to her, she never knew when to stop.

She was debating with herself whether to change another fiver when Damon came along. He wasn't aware that she watched him and there was that vulnerable hurt look again.

He spotted her and grinned. "So this is where you got to! Poor old Guy is rather upset. He thinks you've run out on him."

As Kate looked at him something inside her brain snapped. What were they playing at? No-one as young as Guy was going to fall for a woman ten years older than him and Damon was the captain, for God's sake! The game had gone far enough.

"Now look here," she hissed. "You've both had your little joke at my expense, now you can leave me alone."

He stared in disbelief. "What are you babbling on about?"

"Do I have to spell it out to you, Captain? I bet I'm the laughing-stock of the messroom . . . " She broke off. It really wasn't like her to go on so. She was discovering a lot of hidden traits which quite alarmed her.

He put a hand on her shoulder. "You

really believe that, don't you? You can't accept that you are a desirable woman."

"Ha!" She tried to push him away but it was like trying to push over a brick wall. His jacket beneath her fingers felt sensuously smooth and she could feel his muscles beneath it. The experience sent the blood pounding in her temples and succeeded in disturbing her in a way that was entirely new. "Kindly let me pass." Her voice was shaky and her lips trembled.

Surprisingly, he let her go and stood aside. "I beg your pardon."

She hastened to the lifts and jabbed frantically at the buttons.

There came a clank as the lift started towards her and she grabbed a deep steadying breath, but it sailed by without stopping. She jabbed the button again and once more heard it sail past.

"I'll have to report that." Damon studied Kate's stormy expression. "I've obviously offended you in some way."

"Oh, don't apologise."

He hooked the tip of his finger under her chin sending ripples of consternation throbbing through her bloodstream. "I'm not sure what I'm apologising for."

Where was that lift? thought Kate, shaking her chin free. She couldn't wait here all evening and made for the stairs.

At that moment the loudspeaker crackled: "Will Captain Penrose please contact the entertainments officer. Urgent".

Damon went immediately to the wall phone keeping Kate in his line of vision while he dialed.

Kate slowed her walk so she could listen to his side of conversation.

"What's the trouble, Frank? I see . . . Tell Ingram to go to my office and await me . . . What about the Austrailian? . . . Get hold of Guy. He's in the Mainbrace Lounge . . . And the woman? Hold on, I might be able to solve that one . . . "

59

At that moment the lift opened its doors and Kate rushed in heaving a sigh of thankfulness. She ascended rapidly but, on alighting found herself on the wrong deck. Yes, that piece of machinery would have to be reported. She finally arrived on Montego deck and went along the labyrinth of wide-carpeted passageways to her cabin.

As she turned the last corner she was annoyed to find Damon waiting outside her door, arms folded, one uniformed leg drawn up behind him, his foot flat against the wall. Of course, he must have checked her cabin number during the day and would be familiar with all the short-cuts of the ship.

She ignored him and searched in her purse for her key.

"Kate . . . " He pushed himself away from the wall. "I . . . "

"Please go away!"

"I'm trying to . . . "

"You're impossible!" she snapped. "I've had just . . . "

His hand over her mouth effectively

stopped her flow. "Kate, will you listen? It's your daughter."

He removed his hand and she gasped. "Tamsin?"

"There's been a spot of trouble. She's imprisoned herself in the flag-locker on Dolphin deck. She wants you."

Something inside Kate seemed to crumble and she swayed about on her feet. Coming on top of everything else it seemed like the last straw.

"Hey!" said Damon gently. "Don't you faint on me. I need your help."

She pushed against him irritably. "I'm not the fainting kind."

"Of course you're not." He slipped his arm through hers. "Let's release the poor girl from her self-imposed prison."

The lift worked perfectly for him.

Kate had always found men in uniform intimidating, but Damon was larger than life, tall and broad-shouldered, all buttons and epaulets and gold braid. His presence in that confined space was overpowering.

"What happened?" she asked shakily as they began their descent.

"One of my junior officers got into a scrape with a passenger over your daughter, apparently."

"Sparks?" Kate asked intuitively. "And Harry Brown?"

"Yes, but don't be too alarmed. Jealous rivalry breaks out once a trip on average." Damon's expression darkened and his black brows met. "Though I must admit one of my officers is not usually involved. Young fool! I'll have his stripes for this."

There was a small knot of people outside the flag-locker and they moved aside to let Kate and the captain pass.

"Are you the young lady's mother?" enquired the entertainments officer.

Kate nodded.

He pointed inside the locker to a further door. "She's in there. I guess she's put something over the handle to stop us opening it. She's been crying but she's quiet now." He ushered Kate inside and drew back.

She was in a small room lined with pigeon-holes crammed with rolled-up signal flags. She knocked on the inner door. "Tamsin? It's mum. Please come out, dear."

"Is anyone out there? I can't face them," Tamsin asked in a tiny little voice.

"No, dear." She felt sure Damon would have dispersed them by now.

She heard the sound of something heavy being removed from the other side of the lock. A moment later Tamsin flung herself into Kate's arms.

Kate studied the flushed, tear-stained cheeks. "You look terrible," she remarked gently. "Let's get to our cabin."

Only Damon waited outside. "Okay?" he asked.

"Yes," said Kate, then as an after thought, "Thank you Damon."

He put them in the lift. "Goodnight Kate, Tamsin."

★ ★ ★

"It's all my fault," said Tamsin, sitting listlessly on the edge of the bed. "I feel so ashamed. I should have known what was going to happen."

Kate kicked off her shoes and padded to the dressing table. "What started it?"

"The fight? I don't know." Tamsin caught her breath. "Yes I do! I played them one against the other."

"Tamsin!"

"Oh, not on purpose," Tamsin murmured. "It's only now I can see what I did. To get even with Ronnie, I suppose. Does that make any sense to you?".

"Yes, strangely enough," Kate replied softly. "But you can't take all the blame. Men aren't puppets. They're responsible for their actions. So what happened exactly?"

"I danced with both of them because each insisted." Tamsin's blue eyes clouded. "Then Sparks asked Harry to step outside, just like in the movies. He knocked Harry down and blood was streaming from his nose. His lip was cut too and he's lost a cap from one of his teeth. Sparks was completely unmarked. I just ran away and hid."

"Yes, you always had a habit of doing that."

"Sparks will be in trouble with the captain, won't he?" Tamsin asked tremulously.

"Yes, I think you could say that." Kate carefully removed her gold earrings. "Damon said he'd have his stripes."

Tamsin rose and began to prepare for bed, her lovely face anxious and brooding. "Thanks for rescuing me. I hope it didn't ruin your evening."

Kate pulled a face. "As a matter of fact, you rescued me."

"Poor mum! So we've both been through the wars." Tamsin stared gloomily out of the window. "And poor Harry! I hope Guy Lewis can perform dentistry."

Kate gave a guilty start. "Guy! I

forgot all about him."

Tamsin forced a wan little smile, "Don't tell me you're leading two men on at the same time." She stopped and became thoughtful. "People will say that's what I was doing . . . "

"I'm not leading Damon on," Kate cut in hotly. "And I've told Guy exactly where he stands."

Tamsin sighed. "This is all Ronnie's fault. If he hadn't chickened out of marrying me, none of this would have happened."

3

WHEN Nelson brought the coffee and news-sheets the next morning he stared with undisguised interest at Tamsin. It was easy to see the fight was the main topic of conversation among the cabin crew.

And not only the crew. All eyes were on Kate and Tamsin as they entered the dining-room. Tamsin chose a table in the corner hidden by a potted palm.

A few moments later, Guy Lewis joined them. "How's the *femme fatale* this morning?"

Kate shot him a warning glance. "How's Harry?"

"Not a pretty sight. I've seen to his nose and lip. And I've faxed ahead for him to see a dental surgeon when we arrive in Cozumel."

"And what about Sparks?" asked Kate.

"He's in the brig." He grinned ruefully. "Not literally. He's confined to quarters for the duration of the voyage. He'll be severely dealt with when we return to Miami. Striking a passenger is a serious offence . . . "

"But Harry was equally to blame by all accounts," Kate cut in.

"It makes no difference. Sparks knows the rules."

"It seems so unfair," murmured Kate. "Is Harry lodging a complaint."

"No fear! He feels a big enough fool already."

Tamsin stood up abruptly. "I'm not hungry. And it's stifling in here. I need air."

Guy watched her go. "Poor kid. Still, she's young. She'll get over it. You said she was going through a bad patch. Some fella, I suppose?"

"Yes, some fella."

He leaned across the table towards her suddenly. "Where did you get to last night?"

Kate was annoyed to feel her cheeks

68

growing warm. "I'm sorry, Guy, but I can't take you seriously. Why aren't you chatting up a nice young girl? There are plenty of them about."

He ignored her question and frowned. "I suppose you saw Damon?" He added sourly, rising from his chair, "I wouldn't have thought he was your type."

"How do you know what is my type? You don't know me," she protested. "Anyway I don't believe in classifying people into types."

She accompanied him to the exit where he saluted her. "Enjoy your day! I hope to see you later."

Tamsin was pacing the floor of the cabin when Kate arrived.

"I've been thinking, Mum. You must go to Damon and plead with him to drop the charges against Sparks."

"Me!" Kate laughed mirthlessly. "How do you make that out?"

"He's sweet on you."

"You're not thinking straight. He won't listen to anything I say."

"He will! He will!" Tamsin grabbed

her mother's hands. "If anyone can make him see reason you can."

Kate went to the wardrobe. "I'm sorry, Tamsin, but it won't do any good. Besides the less I see of him the better."

Tamsin's expression clouded. "Sparks is languishing in his cabin and might be kicked off the ship when we get back to Miami. I don't see how you can refuse when all it needs is a word from you to make everything okay again."

"You have more faith in my abilities than I have." Kate's voice was muffled as she rummaged through the hangers. "I don't think Damon will appreciate my interfering with ship matters."

"I feel responsible for the trouble Sparks is in," Tamsin pouted. "Don't you see?"

"Yes, I do see. But I can't interfere."

"Please, Mum. If you do this thing for me I'll never ask for another thing."

"Hm! Where have I heard that before?"

"The whole thing is preposterous,"

70

went on Tamsin. "Locking Sparks up because he lost his temper."

"I agree with you there."

"Then you'll do it?" There was a trace of optimism in Tamsin's tone. "Oh, Mum!"

"You'll wear me down till I agree, won't you?"

Tamsin threw her arms round Kate's neck and hugged her. "Thanks, Mum. I knew you wouldn't let me down."

★ ★ ★

Kate spent the morning ambling round the deck, hoping she might bump into Damon and so save her the ordeal of having to make an appointment to see him. But she was out of luck. It seemed he was only around when she didn't want to see him.

It was mid-afternoon before she decided she must act. She changed into a beetroot teeshirt and a pair of baggy black slacks that didn't draw attention to her spare tyre.

71

She approached the offices they'd had pointed out to them on the tour of the ship yesterday. The open door led to a little ante-room where two seamen sat, one tapping away with one finger at a typewriter, the other operating a telephone switchboard.

She cleared her throat. "Could I . . . possibly speak to . . . the captain?"

"Certainly, Madam," The man at the typewriter inclined his head towards a further door where a large sign read KNOCK AND ENTER. "Just knock and go right on in." Then, seeing her hesitate, "Go on, that's what we do."

"I don't like to." This was utterly ridiculous.

"He doesn't bite. Not passengers anyway." The man stood up and came round the desk. "Okay, I'll take care of it for you."

He rapped efficiently on the door, pushed it open and bellowed, "A lady to see you, sir."

Damon, hatless, jacketless and with sleeves rolled up, was seated behind a large desk cluttered with papers and maps. Behind him shelves full of textbooks lined the wall. It could have been the office of any businessman. There was another door at the far end of the room and Kate surmised it led to his staterooms.

He stood up. "Come on in, Kate. Take a seat."

She placed her clutch bag on the edge of the desk, took a chair facing him and crossed her long legs.

His gaze flickered over her red teeshirt. "What can I do for you, Kate?"

As he sat down again she noticed he had a small anchor tattooed on his left forearm. It seemed to accentuate his masculinity somehow and she felt her stomach shrink into a tight unfamiliar knot. Striving to ignore the weakening affect he had on her emotions, she came straight to the point.

"I've been elected to say a word on behalf of Sparks Ingram."

The eyes which had seemed so benign

a moment earlier hardened. But before he could reply a seaman knocked and entered with a document requiring his signature. He signed with a flourish and the man departed.

"Sparks is very young," she ploughed on, "and he behaved impulsively. Can't you overlook it just this once?"

"No, I can't." Damon leaned his elbows on the desk. "Ingram knows better than to fight with a passenger."

"But it's so unfair. Sparks is in danger of losing his job and Harry Brown gets off scot-free."

"I wouldn't call a busted nose, a cut lip and a cracked tooth getting off scot-free," Damon countered evenly.

"Well, no," she conceded, "but both of them were equally to blame and Dr Lewis assures me that Harry doesn't want to lodge a complaint against Sparks. Surely you can . . . "

Another knock and a young woman in uniform placed a pile of folders in Damon's IN tray and left.

"The discipline of the crew is of

prime importance on this ship," said Damon, "This is not industry where that sort of thing can be overlooked and swept under the carpet."

"I know that . . . "

"Well, stop telling me how to run my bloody ship!"

She flinched.

His eyes softened. "Forgive my language but you see . . . "

The telephone by his elbow rang and he grabbed the receiver. "Don't bother me with such trivialities! See the entertainments officer!" he barked into it and slammed it onto its cradle.

Staring at Kate, he said, "There's nothing I can do."

She changed her tack. "This fight between Sparks and Harry was the result of an emotional conflict." She paused to study him. "Are you always in control of *your* emotions, Captain?"

"Yes, I am. Especially in matters involving women." He ran his fingers through his dense hair. "Good lord! Ingram had only just met the girl. It wasn't as if she was the great love of his life. The young idiot must learn to curb that temper of his."

"You're a hard man."

"Would you prefer a weak captain for your cruise?" He drummed his fingers on the desk. "I'm sorry, Kate, but Ingram doesn't expect to be treated differently from anyone else. Besides, the incident has been logged."

"Can't you unlog it?" she asked hopefully.

A harsh laugh was his answer.

"I thought you'd take that arrogant attitude . . . " She stopped. She hadn't meant to say that. She had no wish to antagonise him.

"So my attitude is arrogant and yours is reasonable? How like a woman!"

She stood up. "There's nothing more to say then."

His grim expression smoothed as he rose also. "Why don't you stay and have a cup of tea with me? It should be arriving any moment now."

"No thanks."

"Aw, come on, Kate. You won't be compromised if that's what's worrying you. It's a little like Waterloo station in here in case you haven't noticed."

As he spoke a junior officer entered and began, "Sir, if you don't get Mr Forbes off my back . . . " He saw Kate and broke off. "I beg your pardon, Madam."

"See me later," said Damon wearily.

"But, Sir . . . "

"Get out, Hammond!"

The man hurriedly retreated and Kate eyed Damon mockingly. "You hard man!"

"Oh, stay and have tea with me," he said impatiently. "Look why don't you make yourself comfortable in the armchair and I'll see what's happened to the steward."

She sighed and gave in. A cup of tea would go down very well. But she moved too quickly and knocked her ankle against the leg of the armchair. "Ouch!"

Damon was at once full of concern.

He lowered her into the chair then went down on one knee before lifting her foot onto the other knee, pulling up her trouser leg and gently massaging her ankle.

His touch sent little shock waves rippling up her body.

A young cadet entered and stood nonplussed at the sight of his senior officer engaged in such an intimate occupation.

"Damn!" muttered Damon. "Go away, Perkins! And turn the sign on the door to say KNOCK AND WAIT."

The young man moved away, his mouth twitching.

"And you can take that grin off your face!"

Poker-faced, the cadet disappeared. They heard him swing the notice around on the other side of the door.

Damon rose to his feet as another seaman burst in. "Sir . . . "

Damon fixed him with a steady gaze.

"How's your eyesight, Stephens?" he enquired drily.

"Sir?"

Damon seized the unfortunate man by the collar and propelled him back throught the door. "See that sign? What does it say?"

"Knock and enter, Sir."

"Look again."

"Oh! Knock and wait. I've never seen that sign before, Sir. Sorry, Sir, I . . ."

Damon cut short the man's apologies and went to address the seamen in the outer office. "The only person I want to see come through that door is my steward with the tea. Is that clear?"

"Yes, Sir."

"And no phone calls." He slammed the door.

Kate tried to hide a grin. "You're very masterful. They're obviously terrified of you."

His lips curved at the corners. "They'd better be!"

He pressed a button on the desk

intercom. "Mac, where's that tea?"

A soft Scottish voice filtered into the room. "Coming, Sir, just warming the pot."

"Make it two cups, Mac."

"Aye aye, Sir."

The steward in question arrived with a silver tray set with fine bone china and a plate of chocolate wafers.

"Really, Mac, aren't you overdoing it?" asked Damon.

"Possibly, Sir."

Mac, in his mid-forties, with craggy features and shrewd grey eyes, was Kate's stereotyped idea of a seasoned mariner. She noticed he wore a thick gold wedding ring.

"You said two cups, not two mugs, so I presumed it was a young lady. You know I like an excuse to bring out the best china, Sir."

"You get more like an old woman every day."

"Oh aye." Mac met Damon's eyes and made a hasty retreat.

There came an urgent knock on the

door, then another. Damon ignored them. "Why don't we take our tea into my stateroom?" he suggested, picking up the tray and heading for the further door.

She rose hesitantly. She didn't want to encourage him but was curious to see where he lived.

She followed him into a large pleasantly-furnished room with a decidedly lived-in atmosphere. She realised he must spend more time here than at his home on shore.

A chess board was set out on a table just inside the door and, from the notes beside it, it appeared he was playing a game with someone in Mexico.

An open bureau was strewn with partially carved models of sailing ships, a penknife and lots of shavings, two mouth organs, assorted seashells, and at least six half-empty packets of Polo Mints. On the top shelf, in pride of place, stood a photograph of an attractive woman with grey hair whom Kate took to be his mother.

One corner of the room held a pile of sports equipment — a tennis racket, a baseball bat, a wet-suit and several fishing rods.

"Will you pour?"

She reached for the heavy silver teapot. "Sugar?" she asked, passing him a translucent cup and saucer.

He nodded. She held the sugar bowl out and watched him take two lumps.

With her own cup in her hand she moved to the bookcase to study its contents, discovering novels by such diverse authors as Innes and Steinbeck, Hemingway and Tom Sharpe; manuals on motortcycling, fishing and gardening; biographies of famous admirals and, surprisingly, several slim volumes of poetry. She read the spines and discovered he liked Keats as well as Ted Hughes.

A music centre nearby contained tapes of Bach, the Beatles and Brubeck. It occurred to her she was being treated to an insight on what made him tick.

There were some photographs on

the wall of Damon on various ships' bridges, their backgrounds ranging from snowcapped mountains to tropical islands.

She came to a silver medal in a glass case. It was engraved 'The Penrose Medal' and she turned enquiring eyes on him.

"My grandfather donated that," he informed her, "to be awarded to the best cadet in his year. I was so proud when I got it. I think that must be my most treasured possession."

"Was it always your ambition to captain a ship?" she asked.

"Yes! I've gone through the whole gamut, from cadet upwards. I've sailed the seven seas in every type of vessel. I've even had to swim for it a couple of times." He grinned easily. "It's a man's life in the Merchant Navy."

She helped herself to a chocolate wafer. "So you're married to your job?"

"You could say that. The s.s. Jamestown Pearl makes a fine bride."

She was reminded of what Guy had

said. "I understand you disapprove of sailors marrying. Why is that?"

"Those who do want the best of both worlds." He walked to the window and gazed out over the shimmering water. "They want the excitement of a career at sea but still expect some poor woman to wait at home for them. How can a man concentrate on his career when his heart's a thousand miles away and his mind's on measles and mortgages? I don't think it's fair on either party."

"Hm! I think I agree with you," murmured Kate. "It must be harrowing being a sailor's wife, having to deal with the measles and mortgages alone, never knowing where her man is, or whether he's alive or dead. It wouldn't suit me."

He turned back to watch her from beneath half-closed eyelids, and she was overcome by an inexplicable surge of excitement.

"I noticed your steward was wearing a wedding ring," she filled the sudden silence. "So he obviously doesn't share your views."

"Oh he's firmly enmeshed in all the trappings of matrimony — children, grandchildren," said Damon.

She wondered if she dared ask about his wife. If she brought the matter up he might think Guy had spoken out of turn. She decided to risk it. "Someone said you were married once."

"Yes," he replied tensely.

"Would it help to talk about it?"

"No, it wouldn't. It was twenty years ago."

And yet you're still affected by it, she thought.

He placed his cup and saucer on the tray and changed the subject. "Are you enjoying your cruise?"

"Yes, very much. The only thing spoiling it is Sparks' incarceration."

"That subject is closed." He put his hand gently on her shoulder. "Well . . . I must get on."

She gazed up into green pools. "And I must go . . . "

She felt powerless to move, mesmerised by his nearness, and a surge of adrenalin coursed through her veins serving to unnerve her to a disturbing degree. Was he going to kiss her?

"Please . . . don't . . . "

"Don't what?" He let her go of her shoulder.

"Oh, never mind." She turned away, almost disappointed and knew she must get away from him before she made a complete idiot of herself.

"I seem to have upset you again." His tone was puzzled. "If you tell me what I've done I'll try to rectify it."

"Upset me?" she asked, her voice brittle. "You couldn't upset me."

His eyes became pinpoints of green light. "Are you sure?"

"Oh, there's no talking to you! I am well aware you find it amusing to play games with me . . . "

"Games?" He looked at her wide-eyed. "You do me an injustice."

She marched abruptly back through

the office and picked up her bag from the desk where she had left it. Then she pushed her way through the knot of seamen waiting outside the door.

They straightened at the sight of her plainly expecting to see their captain hard on her heels. How they jumped to attention, she thought disparingly. Well, she wasn't afraid of him.

Or was she? She slowed her pace outside in the passageway. Wasn't she a little apprehensive of him? Because of the way he could make her feel, because of passions he could arouse in her by his touch?

Kate sought the sanctuary of her cabin as the shafts of panic zigzagging through her gradually subsided. This emotional upheaval was totally new to her. She wasn't sure she was ready for the kind of flirting that seemed to be part of the norm these days. She had known one man and he had been everything to her — husband, lover, protector and friend.

"You're falling apart, old girl," she

muttered, pulling off her clothes prior to showering.

She was sitting in the armchair filing her nails when Tamsin arrived eager for news. "Well?"

"I failed the mission."

Tamsin sank down onto the bed. "Oh no! I was counting on you." She noted her mother's heightened colour. "What happened?"

Kate imparted to Tamsin the less embarrassing details of her interview with the captain.

"Sounds like he fancies you, Mum. Crikey! When I said you should start dating I didn't mean with the captain exactly."

"I wish you'd stop it. The joke's gone far enough."

"What joke?" Tamsin gazed knowingly at Kate. "You really are an idiot. You're a most attractive woman. Just because you're approaching forty it doesn't mean you've got to go around with a sack over your head. Damon's not so dumb he doesn't recognise a decent woman when he meets one."

"Oh, do leave off."

"Now, what are you going to wear this evening?" Tamsin threw open the wardrobe door. "We've got to keep him interested."

Kate decided to go along with the fantasy. It was easier than arguing all the time and it might help Tamsin forget her heartache for a while.

Tamsin selected a shantung suit patterned in broken stripes of cerise and jade. "Hm! We must find a way to jazz this boring old thing up."

"Well, thanks," said Kate indignantly. "That was your father's favourite."

"Exactly."

"Tamsin, I'm too old . . . "

Tamsin grimaced censoriously. "I'm going to make you pay a forfeit every time you say the word 'old'." She went to her own wardrobe and lifted down a black camisole. "This will go beautifully with the suit."

"Oh, I can't wear that. I know it's the fashion but I always think it looks as if you're wearing your underwear."

"Just put it on and get the feel of it. It's real silk."

Kate did as she suggested and had to admit that it did feel good.

Tamsin got down on her hands and knees and groped about under the cupboard. "It's a good thing we wear the same size shoes."

"Oh no." Kate held up her hands. "No way am I going to totter around on your high heels. I'm too heavy."

But Tamsin was a good persuader and presently Kate tottered into dinner clinging to Guy's arm. After the meal they joined Tamsin and Harry in the Mainbrace Lounge for a 'Nostalgia Night' singalong.

The young Australian wore an Elastoplast across his nose, sported an angry bruise at the side of his mouth and displayed a gap in his teeth whenever he smiled. Tamsin was nervous with him at first, blaming herself for his injuries, but he obviously bore her no grudge and gazed at her as adoringly as ever.

The entertainments officer led them through a medley of Stephen Foster ballads and songs from the first world war. They were half way through 'My old Kentucky Home' when Damon, who had been standing at the back of the lounge, left. Gone to get his head down before the middle watch, Kate thought recalling Guy's words.

As they launched into 'Tipperary' a seaman arrived with an urgent message for Guy. Someone had broken a leg in the disco.

"Well, it had to happen," said the doctor. "Have you seen some of the antics they get up to?" He fixed Kate with an intimate look. "I'll be back as soon as I can, sweetheart."

She had no intention of being there when Guy returned. She made her excuses to Tamsin and Harry and ascended to the next deck to play bingo. It was the first time she had ever played and she soon discovered she was too slow to compete with the devotees of the game. Mrs Young showed her what to do and rapidly lost patience with her.

"You must call out quicker. You'll never win at this rate."

It was nearly midnight when Kate returned to the cabin. As she picked up her pyjamas, which Nelson had folded into an elaborate fan-shape, she saw a small package lying on her pillow.

Puzzled, she removed the pretty gift-wrapping and discovered an exquisite lace-edged white handkerchief with the initial 'K' worked in silver thread in one corner. It was similar to those she had seen in the ship's gift shop.

There was a card on which was written in a bold hand: 'Whatever I did to upset you, I'm sorry. Enclosed is my flag of truce.' It was signed 'D'.

Her throat contracted painfully. How would she get him out of her mind if he did things like this?

★ ★ ★

"That's Cozumel," said Nelson, pointing out of the window to a small island, flat and green, beyond which lay the Mexican coastline. "It's a nice little place, only about twenty miles long and still unspoilt. You'll be able to go ashore. Wear flat shoes."

Kate put on a cotton button-through with huge window-pane squares of yellow and brown then stood looking in the mirror.

"They'll see me coming all right," she muttered. "I had my doubts when I bought this dress but you insisted it was okay."

"It is okay," said Tamsin. "It's boldly saying you don't give a toss."

Kate slipped on a pair of white sabots. "But I do give a toss."

"Not today, you don't." Tamsin selected a pair of gypsy hoops and looped them through Kate's ears. "Today you're going to show them."

"That's what I'm afraid of."

Out on the deck, Tamsin said, "You're sure you don't mind my going ashore with Harry? It's just that he's got to see the dentist and wants me to hold his hand."

"You go right ahead. I've arranged to go ashore with the Youngs. They're good company."

"Yes, but they're too old and settled for you. You need someone who's going to jog you out of your rut." Tamsin saw Harry approaching. "I'll sort you out tomorrow."

Kate watched them get into the launch and looked around for the Youngs who were just coming along the deck.

She heard a wolf whistle and saw Guy waving to her from the bridge. He'd already told her he had a mountain of paperwork to clear and couldn't escort her today. He shouted, "A word of advice — don't drink the water."

The harbour was shallow so the ship had anchored a little way off the island and the lifeboats were being put to use as launches. All day they would go back and forth and steps had been assembled on the port side of the ship. It was a precarious business going down them and when Kate reached the bottom she was glad of the seaman's hand. At last she took her seat in the launch crowded with happy laughing passengers.

The water was very clear — the clearest in the world, said Mr Young, who had made a study of their ports-of-call, and it and it seemed to change colour from the deepest indigo to turquoise streaked with aquamarine. Visibility was at least a hundred feet and they could see strange colourful fish and skeletons of old wrecks.

They stepped ashore at San Miguel, a sleepy sprawling town of hotels and supermarkets. An umbrella had been set up on the dock under which two stewards from the ship were preparing to serve coffee all day. A large notice reminded them the last launch would leave at six.

Most of the inhabitants appeared to have Spanish blood but there was a large number of Indians — or

Mayans — identifiable by their fat cheeks, round eyes and short sturdy figures.

Kate and the Youngs joined one of the many minibus sight-seeing tours and were driven several miles south along the beach to the wide open spaces beyond the town.

The driver gave a running commentary in Spanish followed by an English translation and they learned that the area had been inhabited by the ancient Mayans for three thousand years, but little was known about these cultured people who had left behind so many pagan pyramids and murals.

They stretched their legs at Laguna Chancanab, a deep orchid-dredged lagoon, and enjoyed drinks on the very spot where the pirate Henry Morgan had rested between bouts of brigandry.

Back in San Miguel Kate's elderly companions were tired and decided to take it easy for the rest of the day, lolling by the pool of one of the large hotels. It didn't suit Kate and she consulted her programme of events. There was to be a display of local dancing in the main *plaza* at noon.

With some fifty other passengers, Kate stood under the shady palms to watch a troupe perform the fast traditional dances, with music provided by the marimba — a primitive kind of xylophone.

As the last dance came to a frenzied end she glanced idly about her and was startled to see Damon leaning nonchalantly against a wall. It was the first time she had seen him out of uniform and she couldn't help thinking how physically attractive he was in a black sea-cotton shirt and hip-hugging white denims.

His eyes roved over the spectators and, as they lighted on her, she saw him push himself purposefully away from the wall.

She trembled with annoyance. If he attached himself to her now her peaceful day would be ruined.

She pretended she hadn't seen him and slipped into a narrow alley at the side of the plaza. Taking several turnings she came to a little square where the tall buildings shut out the sun and a neglected fountain trickled rusty water into a slimy bowl.

Half a dozen dark-faced black-haired men were squatting on the parapet and rose at her sudden unexpected appearance.

"Ah, *Linda senorita!*" said one, leering at her and displaying a mouthful of broken teeth. "*Bonita rosita!*"

Another reached out and touched her hair. "*Guera preciosa!*"

She began to back away but the men took up positions to block her exit and she staggered into them. As they put out their hands to steady her, she heard their suggestive laughter.

A moment later she was being pushed from one to another of them, their movements getting rougher all the time. "*Please . . .* " She offered her bag to the nearest man. "If it's money you want, take it."

The article was accepted, but the jostling continued.

Kate shivered with terror. She was greatly regretting her impulsive flight from the *plaza*. Even Damon's unwanted company would be preferable to being molested by these men. She had a vivid imagination and was already picturing her body being found in an adjacent doorway.

4

ALL at once there came the sound of running feet and Damon appeared on the scene. Disregarding the fact that he was one against six, he elbowed his way into the throng and grabbed Kate's hand, then said something to the men in Spanish, speaking quietly, illustrating his inbred air of authority that demanded their respect.

As the men fell back, Damon's anxious eyes studied her face. "Are you okay, Kate?" She heaved a great sigh of relief and nodded, drawing strength from the pressure of his warm fingers.

He extended his free hand to the man clutching the tote bag and continued in Spanish, his voice low and compelling. With an ingratiating smile, the man relinquished Kate's property.

Kate was trembling from head to toe

as Damon led her out of the square, through the alleyways and into the bright sunlight.

"What's the matter with you?" His bantering tone could not disguise the concern he had felt for her. "Don't you know it isn't wise to wander off on your own? Mexico is a man's world."

She let go of his hand, feeling her confidence surge back. "I can take care of myself," she said. How humiliating to be rescued from such a galling experience — by him of all people!

"Can you?" he grimaced. "So that's all the thanks I get."

"I didn't ask you to interfere," she protested. "I'd have been perfectly all right."

He gave her an infuriating smile. "Sure you would."

"What did you say to them?" she asked as her curiosity got the better of her.

"That you were my woman."

"Oh!" She shied away, unnerved by his masculine closeness and the intimate look that had crept into his eyes.

He watched her indignant expression and burst out laughing. "Not exactly true, is it? Considering you were running away from me."

She didn't attempt to deny it and forced a smile. They had reached an open air market where the stalls overspilled with strange fruits and vegetables, colourfully woven clothes, exotic flowers and basketware.

Damon said, "Why don't you come and help me choose some material for my mother? I brought some lace the last time I was here, now she needs some silk to go underneath it, for a ball gown." And he fished in his back pocket for a small sample.

"Leave it to me."

For the next twenty minutes she wallowed in the colours and feel of the magnificent materials, inspecting everything on the stall and also demanding to see the materials underneath.

Her final choice was an oyster

shangtung. "It's very expensive. Can you afford it?"

"For my mother? I'll say!" He ordered six yards. With the package tucked under his arm he escorted Kate to the edge of the market. "I only came ashore to get the material, but I don't see any reason to rush back. Have you eaten?"

"No, I thought I'd get a hamburger . . . "

"Would you let me take you to lunch?" He added quickly. "To thank you for your help?"

She hesitated. "I thought we were quits. After all you rescued me . . . " She broke off with embarrassment.

"So you admit I got you out of a tight spot?"

She refused to answer and pivoted on her heel to admire a display of dahlias on a stall beside them.

"They cultivate them here," he said. "Dahlias are indigenous to Mexico." He went to the stall and, after great deliberation, purchased a bunch from the display. They were pale blue with a kind of iridescent sheen. "They're the nearest I could find to match your fascinating eyes."

Kate was disconcerted by his lavish compliment. "Thank you, Damon. They're lovely."

The stall-holder, a wizened crone, cackled, "In Cozumel, when a man gives a woman flowers it means he waits for an answer to his question."

Kate glanced up quickly and felt the heat stealing into her cheeks at the woman's assumption that the two of them were romantically entangled.

A smile tugged at Damon's mouth. "The question was will you have lunch with me?"

The ancient flower-seller went on, "If the answer is yes, then the woman gives him a single flower."

Kate picked up one of the buttonholes around the edge of the display and dug into her purse for the last of her small bills.

"You don't have to do that," Damon

said. "The crafty witch only said it to make a sale."

"I know that!" Kate took the safety-pin from the proffered box. "But I want to."

She attached the flower firmly to Damon's shirt, slipping her hand inside the smooth black material and thrilling to the feel of the thick coarse hair on his chest.

"There's my answer," she said, visibly shaken.

The crone watched them with an intense gleam in her rheumy eyes, then she shot out a scrawny hand and grabbed Kate's arm. "You and this man live together long years. Much happiness."

"Wh . . . what?" gasped Kate.

Damon chuckled. "They like to do a little fortune telling on the side," he explained.

Kate's blush deepened to crimson.

The crone turned her attention to Damon. "This woman give you a fine boy child."

"Yes, yes," he said impatiently, dropping a few coins into her outstretched hand. He grabbed Kate's elbow. "Come on, lets get out of here before she tells us how many grandchildren we're going to have."

Kate, unable to meet his gaze, was utterly disorientated.

"A fine boy child, eh?" he said when they reached the main square. "Kate, your face was a picture."

"I expect it was," she replied haughtily.

"They tell you what they think you want to hear. But I've a feeling she was way off the mark there."

Kate laughed as she saw the funny side. "Way off!"

They reached the forecourt of a car-rental showroom. "You'll let me pay for lunch without any arguments?" he asked suddenly.

"Of course."

"Because I can't stomach shouting matches in restaurants."

"I've never had a shouting-match in a restaurant in my life."

"I know a splendid place on the east coast of the island, about ten miles away, where they serve traditional food," he said. "We'll hire a motorbike."

She laughed shakily. "For a moment I thought you said you'd hire a motorbike."

"I did. Don't be alarmed. It's the best way to get about on Cozumel and I'm a competent motorcyclist."

You would be, she thought philosophically.

The car-rental proprietor agreed to look after their packages and Damon phoned the ship to say he would be delayed.

He selected a powerful-looking Yamaha and wheeled it across the forecourt, then he helped her secure the strap of her crash helmet under her chin.

She pulled on her white linen jacket. "I've never been on a motorbike before."

He sat astride the machine and invited her to climb on behind him.

She slipped the straps of her tote bag round her neck, swung her leg over the seat and tucked her skirt underneath her. The engine sprang to life and she gingerly put her arms around his waist.

They soon left the jampacked town behind and followed a paved road which ran like a seam across the centre of the jungle-mattered island.

Kate, her cheek hard against Damon's broad back, could feel his muscles and sinews straining as he handled the machine.

Within fifteen minutes they had arrived at Punta Morena — a remote outpost which boasted nothing more than a few hotels and restaurants.

They walked towards one of the latter, a picturesque building with blue-tiled roof and Moorish arches, reflecting the Spanish flavour of the island's past.

The decor inside was charmingly simple with stark white walls and marble floor. Flowers were everywhere and the air was heavy with their perfume.

"Ah, *Senor* Penrose!" The head waiter greeted Damon like a long-lost brother. "We are honoured to see you again, Captain." He glanced guardedly at Kate and gave a little bow.

"I suppose you've brought dozens of women here?" she asked Damon as they faced one another across the red tablecloth.

"Dozens!" he agreed lightly, perusing the wine list. "Would you like a Mayan aperitif? I can recommend the *Ixabentum*."

"You're the expert," she acknowledged. "I know nothing about Mexican food. Do you want to order for me?"

"I'll be delighted," he beamed. "We'll begin with the queen-conch cocktail. They're gathered from these waters." His eyes travelled down the menu. "Followed by *conchinita pibil*."

He pushed up his shirt sleeves and she stared once more at the anchor tattoo on his forearm.

He noticed her interest and an irrepressible smile curved his lips. "The result of a teenage dare when I was still at nautical training college."

She tried to picture him as a raw cadet but failed.

She stealthily slipped off her sandals under the table and tasted the aperitif. "Hm! Lovely. It smacks of honey. And there's aniseed in there somewhere."

He ordered a bottle of *Hidalgo*. "Better not get you on the tequila," he observed dryly, "yet."

"And Guy said not to drink the water," she grinned.

He studied her solemnly. "What do you think of Guy?"

There was an edge to his voice and fleetingly she wondered if he resented her friendship with the amiable doctor. The notion sent her pulses galloping erratically. Whatever was the matter with her? All these palpitations belonged to the age of crinolines and high button boots. She took her fork to the queen-conch cocktail. "I think he's very sweet."

"Sweet? Now there's an adjective I hadn't associated with Guy."

For a moment she was tempted to believe he was jealous but commonsense told her this could not be so. Jealousy indicated involvement.

There followed an awkward silence and Kate ransacked her mind for something to break the tension. "I hope your mother likes the material. Do you live with her?"

"No, she lives in Wales with my stepfather. I live in Dawlish. It's a little seaside town in Devon."

"Yes, I know it. My husband and I often went on holiday there." It seemed strange, disloyal almost, talking to this man about Peter. "Go on."

"It's a big old rambling house left to me by my father, with a fine view of the sea. It's been in my family for centuries and I love it, but I don't spend enough time there." He shrugged the wistful moment away.

"So you don't see much of your mother?"

"On the contrary. She and her husband run a charitable trust for disabled children and she's forever roping me in to help out. I arranged for a free cruise for five-hundred of them last year." His eyes danced. "We had a riotous time! Those youngsters wore everybody out!"

"Have you any family besides your mother?"

He shook his head.

"Our steward said you come from a long line of seafaring men."

"Been discussing me, eh?"

She stared at the powerful tanned column of his throat with a sense of fatalism over the events that had led her there. "The captain is always a romantic figure."

"Enough about me," he said gruffly. "Let's talk about you, Kate. Nice name. Is it short for something?"

"Katharine. It means pure and clean." Suddenly she felt foolish and lowered her eyes, wondering desperately about the incredible impact he was having on her. It made no sense. She didn't even particularly like the man. "What does Damon mean?"

"The tamer." He chuckled. "We shall see."

The *conchinita pibil* turned out to be highly-seasoned sucking pig in baked banana leaves, accompanied by beans into which cheese had been stirred. "Delicious," said Kate.

"Yes, they do nice things with beans here."

"Tell me about your father."

"He died in an accident at sea when I was still a kid." His tone and the expression on his face told her they had been very close.

She studied him as he concentrated on his plate. He was easily the most interesting-looking man in the room and there was a positive presence about him — a romantic figure indeed! She experienced a flutter in the pit of her stomach and was immediately on her guard. Her body was warning her to be wary. His gallant behaviour since they had met at midday had lulled her into a false sense of security, but the recollection of the power he seemed to have over her brought her up with a jolt.

She stared at the tattoo and was reminded that he was a seafaring man, a rover. She must have been mad to accept his invitation to lunch. But she had thought they would go somewhere near. She didn't know he was going to bring her to the back of beyond.

They rounded off the meal with rolls of caramel fudge covered with pecan nuts, but Kate hardly noticed what she was eating. Anxious to escape Damon's vital influence, if only momentarily, she took a little mirror from her bag and glanced at her reflection. "I'm going to the ladies' room to freshen up."

As she moved her feet about, feverishly searching for her sandals, he placed a ten-pesos note on the table before her.

"What's that for?"

He looked surprised. "The ladies' room attendant."

She was unable to think straight and raised her voice. "I don't want your money. I pay my own tips."

"Be quiet! I told you I don't like shouting matches."

"Then why behave in that overbearing way?"

"I don't know what you're talking about." He looked genuinely puzzled. "You didn't object to my paying for the lunch."

"That's different." She rose and picked up her bag. "What do you think I am?"

"At this moment?" he enquired. "A bad-tempered shrew!"

His words caught her like a whiplash. She reeled back from him and marched across the floor to the door at the far end.

She rushed inside and leaned against the wash basin, panting heavily. Help! She was nearly forty and acting like a moon-struck teenager. Had the wine gone to her head? Bad-tempered shrew he had called her — and she had to admit he was right.

Offering the note had clearly been a normal reaction to him — a girl mentions the ladies' room and he reaches for his wallet. But it made her feel like some kind of tart.

She splashed cold water on her burning cheeks, wondering how she would ever face him again.

With dismay she discovered she had no small notes in her bag. She had given the last to the flower-seller. If she hadn't bought him that buttonhole she'd have been all right.

She retraced her steps to the table and saw with relief that the ten-pesos note still lay among the assorted plates and glassware.

Damon looked startled as she leaned across him and snatched it up.

She made the long march back to the ladies' room and paid the tip, then swept through the restaurant and out into the sunshine, walking briskly until she reached the car park. She acknowledged it was a futile gesture, there was no-where else to go.

She saw Damon come out of the restaurant and walk slowly towards her. She almost flinched from the angry look in his eyes. Here comes that tempest, she thought.

"I . . . want to go back to San Miguel," she said.

"Don't worry." He picked up the helmets. "You're going back to San Miguel. The sooner I get you out of my hair the better."

She had expected him to take the paved road back to the town and was furious when her veered off onto a rough track through the jungle. They bumped and swayed along for about ten minutes then he halted the machine in a large clearing scattered with ancient stone ruins.

He switched off the engine and threw his helmet onto the ground where it rolled under a thornbush. Then swung his leg over the front of the machine and stood regarding her.

"Why have you brought me here?" she demanded, dismounting and pulling at her chin stap.

"I don't know why, dammit!" He undid the clasp for her and sent the helmet spinning to join its twin.

He placed his hands over her throat and his thumbs absently traced her cheekbones with his fingers. "There's something about you, Kate, that brings out the prehistoric man in me."

She knocked his hands away. "So it's all my fault? Well let me tell you, you leave me totally cold."

"Is that so?" He caught her in his arms. "I've had just about all I'm going to take from you, Kate."

Yes, she thought, he had been remarkably patient with her and all she had given him was aggravation.

His face was dark with anger as he lowered his head.

He *was* going to kiss her. She flinched and closed her eyes. But nothing happened and, venturing to open them again, she was amazed to see another, softer, emotion had entered his expression. When his kiss finally arrived it was unbelievably tender. His lips worshipped hers until her senses swam with the sudden knowledge that she had never been kissed quite like this before.

A feeling of warm languor spread through her veins and she lost total control of her reflexes. The need to respond to his tender advances was too strong to resist and she slipped her hands round his neck, knotting her fingers into his hair.

His lips became demanding, his body a lodestone dragging at her epicentre, sending a tide of pleasure throbbing through her. She arched forward till their bodies were moulded together and a soft moan escaped her lips.

She felt a tremble pass through him before he drew back. Green eyes met blue in a wary exchange.

He shook his head almost in disbelief and slowly his features relaxed. "You have a funny way of showing it," he muttered.

"What?" Even as spoke she knew she shouldn't ask.

"That I leave you totally cold."

"Oh!" Her eyes flew wide open and she struggled against his granite frame, wondering what on earth had possessed her to behave in that abandoned way. "Leave me alone!"

"Hell!" he said, "If ever a kiss didn't go according to plan, that was it. I meant to teach you a lesson, not make love to you." He moistened his lips with his tongue. "I wish you wouldn't do that, Kate."

She gulped. "You wish *I* wouldn't . . . "

"I wish you'd stop messing me about so I don't know whether I'm coming or going."

Her breath caught ragedly in her throat. "So it's still my fault?"

"Just calm down, will you?" He turned away and walked between the untidy heaps of stones. "Come and see the ruins."

With Kate following at a short distance, they walked in silence past the remains of a Mayan pyramid.

When they returned to the motorbike he caught her wrist in a loose grip. "You're a dangerous lady, Kate. I've a feeling any relationship with you could turn serious and I'm not prepared to risk it." He spoke in a light even tone but she detected the subtle undercurrents. "I'm not looking for commitments, especially with a woman as intense as you."

"And I'm not looking for a casual affair with a sailor," she retaliated spiritedly.

He laughed out loud and bent to retrieve the helmets. "Much as I'd like to continue this conversation, I must get back. The Jamestown Pearl sails shortly and it's customary to have the captain on board." He glanced at his watch. "Is that the time? You'll get me keelhauled."

They arrived at the dock just in time to partake of coffee under the umbrella.

The stewards had been lolling about on canvas chairs but sprang to smart activity at the sight of their captain.

The stall was dismantled and stowed on the last shore boat, then Damon handed Kate aboard and they stood in the bows with the spindrift in their faces.

Kate preceded him up the long gangway and observed the veiled glances exchanged between the officers of the watch at the sight of Damon's buttonhole, crushed and wilted by now. He handed his package of material to a steward.

"Thank you for lunch," said Kate humbly. "Sorry I was so prickly."

"I wouldn't have missed it for the world," he rejoined dryly.

Tamsin was not in the cabin but the lids were off several jars of makeup, indicating she'd been and gone.

After that large lunch, Kate decided to forgo dinner and attend instead the Pizza Party being held on Savoy deck at midnight.

She showered, wrote a few postcards and tried to read, but it wasn't easy. It had been a day of shifting moods. She had been stirred to a strange awareness of latent yearnings by Damon's kiss, never having dreamed she was capable of such intense feelings towards a virtual stranger. The last thing she wanted was to become involved with a man like that. She was never going to see him again and had no intention of losing her head — or her heart — over a casual shipboard encounter. She was confident he didn't want to get involved with her either. He had been joking when he pointed out the danger of their relationship becoming serious but she recognised the truth behind the cynicism.

She was still foundering in the magnetic forcefield of his kiss, but she knew that to spend any more time with him would be the height of folly. It could destroy her sane life and rob her of her new-found independence, for the deeper she sank in such an association the harder the parting would be.

★ ★ ★

Kate spent the whole of the following day avoiding Damon and Guy, hiding in her cabin for hours on end and shrinking from every man in uniform, but only succeeded in making herself miserable. By ten o'clock she was suffering from nervous exhaustion and settled for an early night.

The island of Jamaica appeared on the horizon soon after dawn. As the s.s. Jamestown Pearl approached Kate could see brown, green and mauve mountains rising from the black sea — shark-infested, Nelson had informed them gleefully. Soon they were sailing past dusky grey beaches to enter Kingston harbour and berth alongside the pier in the heart of the city.

Tamsin was fixed up with Harry for the day ashore so when, at breakfast, Guy invited Kate to go ashore with him she accepted. She couldn't bear to go through another day like yesterday.

Besides she was confident she could handle Guy.

She had donned her wine and black striped culottes with a matching crepe de chine blouse — another doubtful buy — and was putting on her Scholl sandals when he arrived to collect her.

He whistled. "You look great."

She dabbed Tamsin's 'Je Reviens' stopper to her wrists and behind her ears and ran her eyes over his beige linen shorts and chocolate-brown tee-shirt which set off his lean figure. "You look rather elegant yourself. How did you manage to get the day off?"

"I've an excellent senior nursing sister and I've left her in complete control." He wrinkled his brow. "All the same I was surprised when Damon agreed to my request for shore leave. I made no secret of the fact that I was escorting you."

As they went along the deck and down the gangway to the pier a steel band was entertaining the disembarking passengers with lively calypso music.

There was a reminder to be back on board by eight.

They walked through the dock gates just in time to see Damon, at the wheel of a white Mercedes, drive through. At his side was the strikingly-lovely redhead.

"I've seen her on board," Kate murmured.

"Yes, she's the Honourable Esmeralda Fenshawe," said Guy obligingly, watching the car pass under a row of blue lignumvitae trees. "As she's a Very Important Passenger it's part of his duty to escort her. Some duty!"

They boarded a ramshackle coastal bus which took them through a dozen little towns and villages, passing crops of rice, tobacco, bananas and citrus fruits. As they rounded the island Kate noticed the black sea changing to topaz on the east coast and then blue on the north.

Guy pointed out the landmarks to her — the Rio Grande, the pretty harbour at Port Maris and the misty

Blue Mountains.

At each stopping place the scent of lillies wafted through the open windows along with a strong peaty odour which Guy said was the unique smell of Jamaica. Kate was enchanted to see orchids winding round the trunks of trees and emerald-green lizards basking in the sunshine.

The atmosphere was permeated with the sound of music and singing. "They all seem so cheerful," mused Kate, "Despite their violent history."

"Yes," agreed Guy. "The Jamaicans have survived slavery and earthquakes and they still keep on singing. The pirates once brought in their loot to sell to the merchants and the streets here thronged with drunken roistering seamen." He grinned. "That's why there are so many different coloured skins around."

"Hm! Sailors have a lot to answer for, one way or another," Kate couldn't resist saying.

Ocho Rios was in the tourist belt and

splendid hotels rose majestically from clumps of stately mahoganies, strongly scented cedars and gothic bamboos. Great tree-ferns filtered the sunlight giving welcome shade to the humming birds, their long black tails whirring noisily as their red beaks ripped at the blossoms for honey.

The bus set them down beside an idyllic white beach already peopled with sunworshippers and Kate gazed with delight at the bay of deep-blue water fringed with palm trees.

"It's just as I always pictured it," sighed Kate.

"Yes, not exactly Yarmouth."

"I won't hear a word against Yarmouth," she retorted. "I've spent some of the best holidays of my life there."

"I beg its pardon."

Guy bought tickets for the pay-beach and they trudged over the hot sand to a little circle of changing tents.

As Kate put on a black one-piece bathing suit, she was very conscious of her spare tyre which showed up even though the costume had a built-in girdle. She stared in horror at the varicose vein in her leg and wished she'd thought to bring the cover-up cream, but she hadn't considered it too bad till she'd seen the young nubile girls cavorting on the beach. Well, if he didn't like it he shouldn't have invited her, she thought defiantly, stepping out of the tent. He was a doctor after all and must know what a mature woman looked like.

All the same she held her hat over her abdomen as she emerged from the tent.

Guy appeared dashing and athletic in a brief pair of trunks, his body attractively sprinkled with ginger freckles, the hair on his chest as fiery as that on his head.

He turned admiring eyes on her. "You look ravishing."

She was acutely embarrassed. "You don't have to say that."

"Yes, I do, because it's true."

"Haven't you got someone nice to take to the beach?"

"Yes, I've brought her."

"I mean someone young."

He took her hands and looked at her seriously. "What is all this? You seem obsessed with your age."

"Oh, don't you start. I get enough of that from Tamsin."

He released one of her hands and guided her towards a beach umbrella made of straw. There was a rough-hewn wooden table underneath and some canvas chairs. "I've hired this for the day."

She dropped into one of the chairs. She didn't feel so conspicuous sitting down. "I know men aren't interested in women over twenty-five, so save your breath."

"Is that so?" He burrowed in his holdall and produced a bottle of suntan oil. "Here, anoint me."

She dropped to her knees beside him. "It doesn't matter how preserved an older woman is, men just don't see her as a sex object."

"You're talking rubbish." He lay face down on his towel.

She poured a generous amount of oil into her palm and smoothed it over his back. "So aerobics and face-lifts are a complete waste of time."

He sat up suddenly and seized her shoulders. "You don't know what you're talking about."

And before she knew what he was doing he was kissing her long and hard.

She was flustered and didn't know what to do with her hands so she kept them by her side.

"Did that feel as if I wasn't interested in you?"

"N . . . no."

"Listen." He took up the bottle of lotion and began to apply it to her shoulders. "When I first became ship's doctor, it was Christmas every day. The girls just threw themselves at me. It was like putting a mouse in charge of the cheese."

Kate was even more embarrassed by these revelations and was frightened of what he might say next. She stood up and began to walk towards the ocean.

He bounded after her intent on getting it off his chest. "I never said no. I indulged all my randy fantasies. The trouble with working in a sweet shop is you can make yourself sick," he finished, thoroughly mixing up his metaphors.

She splashed into the warm water and tried not to listen. But she wasn't a very strong swimmer and liked to keep within her depth.

He swam near to her and shouted above the happy noise of the other bathers. "You can see why I've become selective."

There seemed to be no answer to that so she said nothing.

Presently they ran back up the beach to lie on the towels.

She had been thinking how simple was their relationship — a man and a woman enjoying each other's company with no turbulent undercurrents. But she could see she was wrong. It was impossible apparently to have that sort of liaison.

At mid-day Guy went to the restaurant on the promenade, returning with a picnic meal consisting of sandwiches, some strange-looking fruits and several cans of soft drinks.

"What a congenial profession you have!" Kate exclaimed. "There can't be many jobs which allow for lolling about on sunkissed beaches."

"Yes, I'm lucky," he agreed. "These past three years have been rather special." He ripped the ring-pulls off two cans. "I was on the Alaskan run before this, cruising between ranges of snow-capped mountains. Very remote and picturesque in an awesome sort of way, but too cold for me. I wouldn't have applied for it but for my friendship with Damon. We met years ago in the South Pacific and I've always managed to enlist on the same ships as him." He took a swig of Pepsi. "Changes may be ahead though. The company has bought a new ship, the ultimate in luxury, and intends to operate a Scandinavian run. It's a totally new concept in cruising — mini-cruises for businessmen wanting to advertise and exhibit their wares to prospective clients and take orders. Damon's put in for the captaincy, but there are two others in the running, both seasoned captains and both related to senior directors! If Damon gets it I shall apply for the post of medico, naturally."

Kate was quiet, digesting this piece of information.

"Oh-oh, there I go with my big mouth again," groaned Guy. "Damon won't be pleased." His eyelids dropped. "I'm thankful he's occupied with the Honourable Esmeralda today. It was planned all along. She's the daughter of one of the directors and she wants to visit an ancient aunt who lives on the north coast. Otherwise I've a feeling he'd be muscling in on us here."

"And what makes you think that?"

"Come off it!"

"I wish you'd stop teasing me about the captain. He's not interested in me."

"Have it your way."

Guy peeled what looked like a grey lemon and placed it on Kate's paper plate. "This is a sapodilla, but the Jamaicans call them naseberry plums."

She took a spoonful of the soft orange-coloured flesh and was at once reminded of the taste of apricots.

Next Guy cut open a bright red kind of apple and showed her how the pips were set in star formation. He diced the fruit and mixed it with oranges then passed the plate to her. "Star-apples on their own are considered insipid," he explained, "But served with oranges they taste okay. Ideally they should have wine poured over them, then the dish is called 'matrimony'." He grinned. "Damon thinks that's the nearest sailors should get to the subject."

More sunbathing and swimming followed.

Later Kate was lying down under the umbrella when she sensed someone looking at her. She opened her eyes and lifted her straw hat.

Smiling down at her, with the Honourable Esmeralda standing a few paces behind her, was Damon.

5

KATE sat up quickly and reached out to tap Guy's shoulder. "We've got company."

Guy opened one eye and closed it again. "Oh no! What did I tell you? Never speak in jest lest it comes true." He raised himself on one elbow and adjusted his sunglasses. "What do you want, Damon?"

Damon ignored the question. "Well, there's a coincidence!" he exclaimed. "Fancy you picking the same beach as us!"

"Amazing, isn't it?" said Guy. "I wish I hadn't mentioned the beach where I was taking Kate now."

"Oh, did you mention it?" asked Damon. "I'm afraid I wasn't listening."

"Is that so?"

Damon shielded his eyes and looked about him. "I see all the umbrellas have gone. May we share yours?"

"Can I stop you?"

"Very decent of you."

When Damon and Esmeralda had gone to the changing tents, Guy sat up and clasped his knees. "That does it! I'll swing for him yet!"

"But maybe it was a coincidence . . ." said Kate. "Perhaps he wasn't listening . . ."

"Oh he was listening all right. I know him. I don't know why he's brought Esmeralda with him." His face scowled as a thought struck him. "Unless it's to palm her off on me!"

"I think you're over-reacting," murmured Kate.

When the other two returned to the table, both had on swimwear, Esmeralda a brief green bikini which suited her colouring and showed off her curvaceous figure to perfection, Damon a pair of black trunks, a trifle too tight.

Kate could not take her eyes off him. His body was already tanned and the light smothering of coarse hair on his chest was dark and curly.

She saw him watching her in turn and promptly placed her hat over her spare tyre. He smiled to himself and she blushed. Then she thought no, why should I hide all my figure faults? They can take me as they find me. She deliberately dropped the hat and lay down full-length again.

Esmeralda sat at the table and asked Damon to oil her back. As he did so she giggled and squirmed like a teenager. Kate wondered how old she was and decided she couldn't be much more than twenty-five. It was a depressing thought.

When it was Esmeralda's turn to anoint Damon, after just two strokes of the redhead's hand, Kate jumped up and went down to the water's edge.

She was joined by Guy. He caught her hand and said, "Couldn't you bear to watch that gorgeous creature move her hands over Damon's body?"

Oh dear, was it so obvious? Is that

what Damon would think? She was no good at this game. It was all too subtle for her.

"Why did he have to come here?" Guy sounded extremely annoyed and who could blame him? thought Kate. It was too bad of Damon.

They went for a swim and when they came out and walked back up the beach the oiling was completed, much to Kate's relief.

In the middle of the afternoon Damon went off to the restaurant and returned with a carrier bag which he placed on the table. "Help yourselves," he invited.

It contained seafood — shrimps, prawns, lobster meat, scampi and tiny anchovies. There was also a packet of brown bread and butter and the usual condiments.

Guy arranged the chairs around the table and they sat down to enjoy the feast.

Kate was seated next to Guy with Damon opposite and she was so afraid of touching the latter's bare knees with her own that she sat with her legs leaning as far away as possible — only to come into contact with Guy.

He, plainly thinking she was playing footsie with him, gave her an intimate smile. She felt trapped.

Guy asked after Esmeralda's aunt.

"She's fine!" replied the redhead. "Getting older, naturally, but she still manages to get about." She turned, to Damon. "It was awfully sweet of you to drive me. Your time must be at a premium."

"It's always a pleasure to drive a beautiful young lady about," he replied gallantly.

"Why, thank you, Damon." Esmeralda positively glowed and she cast a smug glance at Kate.

Kate looked away. She hadn't realised she and the redhead were vying for Damon's attention. And she didn't want to see Damon flirting with Esmeralda. Was she jealous of the lovely girl? Because she was young?

She rather thought she was.

She relaxed her legs and immediately came into contact with Damon. Oh, she thought with exasperation, there's no way I can win here.

She rose and stretched. "I think I'll go and change."

"Oh, already?" asked Guy.

"I'm sorry, I can only take so much sun."

"Okay." He turned to Damon and said gleefully, "Sorry to break up the party."

The two men looked at each other like a couple of warring dogs then Damon shrugged. "See you later then."

Kate and Guy went to the tents, but when they emerged fully clothed they saw Damon and Esmeralda coming over the sand towards them.

"We thought we might as well leave too," said Damon easily.

"I must go and put some make-up on," said Kate. "Where's the ladies room?"

Guy pointed it out and took from

his wallet a small note which he held out to her. "For the attendant," he said.

Kate had forgotten this small courtesy and was taken aback somewhat. What should she do? Make a fuss as she had before? Or take the note and say nothing?

Damon was watching her, a sardonic smile on his face.

She smiled at Guy, took the note and marched away.

She was putting fresh lipstick on before the mirror when the door opened and Esmeralda came in also clutching a note.

"That's a nice shade, what is it?" she asked.

"Oh," Kate checked the base of the lipstick case. "It's *Tropical Rumba*. What's yours called?" she added politely.

"*Sailors' Delight*. It's a new shade." Esmeralda ran the bright pink lipstick boldly round her generous mouth. "It's kissproof, I'm assured." She gave a little laugh. "Of course I haven't tried it out on Damon yet. But it'll have to be something special to withstand his kisses." She looked slyly at Kate. "Or wouldn't you know about that?"

Kate blushed and, pretending she hadn't heard, went swiftly into a cubicle.

When she came out Esmeralda was still there.

"Is there something going on between you and the captain?" she asked Kate bluntly.

"N . . . no."

"You don't sound too sure." Esmeralda straightened her skirt. "Only I like to see what the competition is." She studied Kate in the big mirror and gave a little shrug as if there was nothing for her to worry about.

Kare was incensed but she kept her temper, "Don't bother about me," she said icily. "I wouldn't have him for all the tea in China. You're welcome to him." And she picked up her bag to search for a handkerchief. She found Damon's flag of truce.

Esmeralda stared at it. "So you're the one he was buying that for."

Kate was startled. It indicated that Esmeralda and the captain had gone shopping together. Unless the redhead had just happened to be there at the same time and was making capital of it. Ah, thought Kate, perhaps I am learning the rules of this game after all. She smiled at Esmeralda, paid the attendant and left.

Damon and Guy were perched on a low wall waiting for them.

"Well," said Guy in a brisk manner. "We'll be off. We're going to take a taxi back to the dock. I want to take the long way home to show Kate Fern Gully."

"Oh, there's no need to order a taxi, I'll drive you," said Damon walking towards the car park where he had left the Mercedes. "No trouble at all."

Kate felt sorry for Guy and said quickly, "I wanted to buy some souvenirs in that little shop on the promenade."

"Go ahead," said Damon. "We'll wait."

Kate and Guy strolled up to the promenade where Kate poked about in the souvenir trays, taking her time in the hope that the others would get tired of waiting, although she didn't really think it would happen.

"He's sticking to us like glue," observed Guy with a sour look on his face.

"I'm so sorry, Guy, he's spoiled your day."

He placed an arm around her shoulders. "Yes, and there are not so many of them left."

"Perhaps we can ditch them in Kingston."

"I hope so."

When Kate could stall no longer she bought a headscarf with local flowers on it and several miniature pottery folklore animals — Moos-Moos the mouse, Kisander the cat and Bredda Tiger.

They went back to where Damon

and Esmeralda were waiting and Kate saw that Damon had a streak of *Sailor's Delight* on his cheek.

Guy immediately cheered up. "You've been at the jam," he said, whereupon Damon took out a handkerchief and wiped his face.

Esmeralda whispered to Kate, "Not kissproof at all."

They all piled into the Mercedes, Damon and Esmeralda in the front and Kate and Guy in the back.

Damon drove south through the beautiful deeply-shaded Fern Gully and across a plateau, before coming to the steep hairpin bends of Diablo Pass, a breathtaking experience which had Kate on the edge of her seat with excitement and trepidation.

She held on to Guy's hand tightly. At one point he leaned across to kiss her but the car gave a sudden swerve and he missed.

"Sorry," said Damon, "There was a pothole."

Suspecting he had done it on

purpose, Kate stared at the back of his head and then in the rear-view mirror at him. He caught her looking and winked. She took it to mean he had swerved the car deliberately and she glared at him, hoping she conveyed her disgust.

They arrived at the dock and Damon suggested a ride in an open-topped horsedrawn bus.

Guy began to protest but Damon insisted.

"Kate will love it."

It was in with the regular bus service and the picture of it at the terminus reminded Kate of the old-fashioned charabanc rides her mother had told her about. She enthused about it before she remembered her suggestion that they should ditch the other two.

They joined the queue along with a great many others for 'the round trip' — a tour of the harbour area, but when the vehicle arrived there was a great deal of shoving and Kate and Esmeralda were pushed to the back.

"Guy, you jump on board and I'll pass the ladies up to you," yelled Damon.

"Good idea," said Guy, leaping onto the platform.

Damon manhandled the giggling Esmeralda into Guy's arms and then turned to grab Kate. As she reached out her arms to Guy the conductor shouted that the bus was full and was leaving.

Kate was almost aboard, just one more stretch and she would be in Guy's arms.

"Quickly!" she cried.

"Push her nearer!" yelled Guy.

Kate braced herself for a little extra effort. Then to her utter amazement she felt a check on her movements. Damon was definitely holding her back. She tried to wriggle out if his grasp but he had her in a firm grip. "Sorry!" he shouted to Guy.

The bus moved away and Guy looked as if he was contemplating jumping off.

"Stay on!" shouted Damon. "Look

after Esmeralda!"

Kate watched the bus disappear round the corner with two faces staring back at them in bewilderment.

"You did that on purpose!" stormed Kate. "Oh, how could you!"

"Did what?" Damon's eyes were wide with innocence.

"You held me back."

"Well, if you choose to think that . . . "

"I do."

He shrugged.

"They'll get off at the next stop."

"No they won't," he said calmly. "They'll have to do the round trip. They'll be about an hour."

She watched him circumspectly, suspecting he had engineered the whole thing.

"What would you like to do now?" he asked.

"With you? Nothing!" she snapped.

"Oh come on." He looped her arm through his and led her across the road to a bar with the word KARAOKE written on the window.

Kate sulkily allowed him to buy her an apperitif and sat there on the shady terrace glowering at him.

"I wish you wouldn't look at me like that. Look I'm sorry we got separated from the other two but what do you expect me to do about it?"

"I think you played a dirty trick on Guy."

"Oh, let's drop the subject. Can you sing?"

"A little. I was in the school choir — many moons ago . . . " She stopped. "Now wait a minute."

He pulled her out of her chair. "Come on."

He dragged her inside and up to the bar where he had a word with the disc-jockey. A moment later he and Kate were on the little platform with microphones in their hands.

"Oh, I can't do this," said Kate horrified.

"Too late now."

She looked up at the television screen and saw the words 'You made me want to hold you.' She badly wanted to leave the stage but there were several people there from the ship and she didn't want to look foolish. And she *did* know the tune.

She began croakily but soon got into her stride — and Damon was singing along with her.

He had a deep baritone voice and complemented her soprano. They were singing a very romantic song and gazing into each other's eyes.

As the song came to an end Damon leaned over and kissed her, first on her cheek then on her lips.

They received a huge round of applause and Kate realized she had enjoyed it. So much so that when the disc-jockey suggested they sing another she was all for it.

They were singing their fifth duet when Guy and Esmeralda walked in.

Guy, his eyes blazing, stood clenching his fists. "I'm glad you managed to enjoy yourselves while we went on the round trip."

Damon got down from the stage then turned to hand Kate down. "The thing is did you enjoy your trip?"

"It was wonderful." Guy muttered something to Damon and Kate caught the words "swing for you".

He reached for Kate's hand and pulled her towards him. "Come on, sweetheart, we're going somewhere — on our own." When they were out of earshot he muttered, "I told you he was going to dump Esmeralda on me."

* * *

"This trip is turning out to be a dead loss," said Guy broodingly as they sat in the bar of the famous Stony Hill restaurant, where they had a panoramic view of the city of Kingston. "Apart from the fiasco today, it's the sixth day out and I'm getting nowhere with you."

Kate, grinned apologetically. "Why don't you give up while there's still time to try your luck elsewhere?"

"I'm not one to change horses in

midstream," he said stubbornly. "Once I've chosen then that's it."

"But did you choose me? I thought we were thrown together accidently when Tamsin asked Sparks to bring along a fourth."

"No accident! I was mightly attracted to you when you came aboard the first day. Even though you only had eyes for Damon."

She stared at him indignantly. "Oh, that's not true . . . "

He ignored her interruption. "So when I heard young Sparks was looking for a fourth I made sure I was your man."

Kate's expression softened. "Did you?"

Time was getting on and they made their way to the dock.

A young nurse was waiting for Guy at the top of the gangplank and she ran forward anxiously. "Oh, Doctor Lewis, that ulcer in cabin D33 is causing a few problems."

Guy groaned. "The Fates seem

determined to keep us apart, Kate. I'll see to this matter and come along to your cabin later, shall I?"

"No!" She said quickly adding, "I'd rather . . . you didn't . . . "

He gave her hand an urgent squeeze. "Kate, gimme a break!"

She trembled. "I have . . . a headache."

"I can prescribe something for that."

"No . . . thanks, I'd like to be alone. I think I'll miss dinner."

She thanked him for taking her out and walked smartly away.

As she went downstairs she went over incidents of the disturbing day. So Damon had kissed that beautiful young lady. And he was probably with her now. Kate couldn't deny the angry wave of jealousy that raged through her. It was a physical pain destroying her reason. Let her have him, she thought, the Honourable Esmeralda Fenshawe was welcome to him. But the force with which she mustered the words was not as potent as hitherto.

She must definitely pull herself together or she was heading for a breakdown.

★ ★ ★

Kate zipped into her yellow flying-suit and went off to play bingo again. At a few minutes to midnight she made her way back to her cabin, poorer by several pounds, in spite of Mrs Young's guidance.

Kate was halfway along the deck when she heard a low whistle behind her. She turned to see Damon and wondered what inner sense had led her there when she knew full well it was his habit to walk to the bridge around that time.

"All alone?" he asked. "Where's Guy?"

"I've no idea," she said lightly, countering, "Where's Esmeralda?"

His eyes gleamed with idle humour. "She comes under the heading 'duty' so there's no need for you to be jealous of her."

"Jealous?" Kate echoed. "Well, really!" But she recalled the emotions which had plagued her when she had seen him and Esmeralda in the Mercedes and a wave of guilt swept over her.

"You were wearing her lipstick." She bit her lip. She hadn't meant to say that. It made it sound as if she cared.

He chuckled. "As a matter of fact she kissed me."

"Oh yes?"

"I have no designs on Esmeralda. Kate, you are an idiot." He paused. "But a very beautiful one. That suit thing you're wearing is sensational."

"Thank you." She wanted to believe him, about Esmeralda.

Eight bells sounded nearby. He said suddenly, "Share the watch with me!"

"Share the watch?" She viewed him with suspicion.

"Yes, come on the bridge with me."

"No, thanks." What a rash idea!

"Come on! You'll find it facinating, I'm sure. What are you frightened of?"

"I haven't forgotten that dirty trick you played on Guy this afternoon."

"I didn't do anything. You can't expect me to have any control over the country's transport system." He laughed. "And as for holding you back, you must have imagined that."

"I know what I know."

"Aw, come on, Kate, join me on the bridge. I won't be able to get up to any dirty tricks there." A slow smile wreathed his lips. "We'll have at least three sailors on watch with us. What do you say?"

Her defences were down now. Rash or not, the idea appealed to her. "I'm tempted."

"Well, give in to temptation."

She mused, what the heck! "Okay then."

Help! Her stomach twisted into a tight knot. Now what was she letting herself in for? Why couldn't she leave well alone?

★ ★ ★

As Kate stepped over the threshold of the bridge she was aware that four pairs of eyes were watching her.

"Mrs Ashley is joining us," Damon said and the three seamen exchanged sly grins.

"You might as well get your head down, Grant," Damon addressed the officer of the watch. "I'm taking over."

"Thank you, sir."

There were angled lights over the complicated-looking instruments and charts, giving an eerie greenish glow to the area and casting shadows in the corners. The helmsman stood in the middle of the floor and the other two men were positioned by the windows.

"They're the lookouts," said Damon.

Kate dropped into a king-sized leather chair. "Is this yours?"

"Yes. The Captain's Chair. Very prestigeous."

She examined the instruments before her. "It's like mission control."

He sat down on a bench behind

an opaque glass wall partitioning off the radar equipment and patted the seat till she joined him. "It's a long way to our next port of call, Great Inagua. We arrive at seven o'clock sharp tomorrow."

Kate listened to the steady hum of the engines and the intermittent clicking of the instruments and felt herself unwinding.

"Will we be here all night?" she asked yawning.

"That's the general idea. Though by the look of you I doubt if you'll make it."

One of the lookouts disappeared for a few minutes to return with steaming mugs of tea which he passed round.

Kate cradled her mug in her hands and studied Damon's face so close to her, taking in the strong jawline and the brooding gaze in his eyes.

"Do you make a habit of bringing women here?"

"No, it isn't encouraged. You're the first."

A lookout said, "Red light on the starboard bow, sir."

Damon rose and walked to the window. "Starboard five degrees. One short blast," he ordered.

"Starboard five degrees, one short blast, sir," said the helmsman.

Kate heard the hooter sound and felt the slight redirection of the ship.

Presently the helmsman said, "Five degrees to starboard, sir."

"Very good," said Damon. More minutes passed then, "Port five degrees."

"Port five degrees, sir."

"'Midships."

"'Midships, sir."

"Steady."

"Steady, sir."

Damon returned to the bench and pulled Kate's sleepy head against his shoulder. It was an essentially tender action and she was content to remain there within the comfort and strength of his arms.

"Why does the helmsman repeat everything you say?" She yawned again.

"So I know he understood my instructions."

"And what was all that about?"

"A ship coming across our bows from the right — or starboard as we say," he explained. "We are obliged to give way. Green light to port keeps clear of us."

She sighed. "It sounds very involved. Is the sea your friend?"

He laughed. "That's romantic nonsense! The sea is always the enemy."

During the next hour or so Damon was constantly called on to navigate. He spent long moments pouring over the instruments and charts and made several entries in the log, always returning to Kate's side.

The atmosphere throughout was one of easy camaraderie. The seamen laughed together and exchanged nautical small-talk with their captain, most of which was incomprehensible to Kate.

She found it increasingly difficult to keep her eyes open and eventually slumped against Damon's shoulder. At once she felt his powerful arms around her, gathering her up and carrying her swiftly to an iron door at the side of the bridge.

"Keep her steady, Jim," he told the helmsman.

The man allowed his eyes to sweep over Kate's inert form and a slight smile etched his lips. "Keep her steady, sir," he repeated.

Kate giggled.

"You're undermining my authority." Damon carried her into a small utility cabin, flicked on the light and kicked the door shut. "This is my sea cabin."

It was sparsely but adequately furnished with a narrow bed and a kind of tallboy that served as a wardrobe, a dresser and a wash-stand.

As he set her down gently on the edge of the bed, alarm swept away the hazy wanderingings of her mind. "Why have you brought me here?"

He perched beside her and smoothed her hair from her forehead, a singularly tender gesture that set her nerves jangling again.

"I just wanted to kiss you goodnight before I detail someone to escort you back to your cabin," he explained. "Where's the harm in that?"

She made a movement to rise but his hands on her shoulders restrained her, then his lips dropped to hers in a burning kiss that dealt destruction to any further resistance she might offer.

As his mouth lingered on hers she experienced a primitive pulse deep within her which lifted her spirits to a state of euphoria. The feeling trickled its way through her veins bringing with it a gnawing pang of desire.

"Kate!" Damon gave a self-deprecating chuckle. "I'd like to stay, but I've dismissed the officer of the watch and can't desert the bridge."

As he spoke there came a tap on the door and one of the lookouts called, "Red light on the starboard bow, sir."

Damon raised his voice. "Very good." Then softly, "Stay here, Kate. I'll be back in a moment."

Directly he had gone, Kate jumped to her feet. She must be mad!

She tried the handle of a second door at the far end of the cabin. It was unlocked and led to the passageway, thus sparing her the embarrassment of having to pass through the bridge.

She sped back to her cabin and slipped in quietly so as not to wake her daughter.

As she prepared for bed a quavering sigh escaped her throat and treacherous thoughts invaded her mind. If she were honest with herself she had to admit she had thrilled to Damon's kiss, had wanted to stay in his arms.

With an effort she pulled herself together. She had already decided that a casual relationship was out. And what could be more casual than a shipboard romance? He already meant too much to her and the only course of action now open to her was to resist his obvious attraction in future and *stay out of his way*.

And yet . . . that breathless emotion which had so overwhelmed her had left her with an enchanting ache.

She climbed in under the duvet, smiling crazily up at the ceiling for long minutes before sleep overtook her.

★ ★ ★

Great Inagua Island loomed out of the sea the next morning, all green and fresh, as if it had been especially aired for them. It was at the end of the Windward Passage, a Bahaman island in the West Indies Group with a population of just over a thousand.

"Where did you get to last night?" Tamsin was propped in the armchair, one foot on the seat as she painted her toenails.

Kate climbed out of bed, stretching and yawning. "Gosh! I'm so tired. I shared the middle watch with Damon."

"You're kidding!"

"No, straight up. It was fascinating." Kate gazed pensively out of the window.

She could see a mass of land on the horizon behind them that was the eastern tip of Cuba. She glanced at her watch. Seven o'clock. "How does he do it?" she muttered to herself.

"I think he's falling for you," murmured Tamsin.

"Don't be silly. He's not the kind to fall."

Tamsin stopped what she was doing and gazed up at her mother. "Are you falling for him?"

"I don't know," Kate replied slowly. "I haven't felt like this in a long time. Perhaps never."

"Oh-oh!" muttered Tamsin. "Woman overboard!"

Kate trailed her fingers through a pile of pottery pieces on the dressing table and changed the subject. "You bought a lot of souvenirs yesterday."

"Oh, Harry bought those for me. I like him, a lot, but I keep thinking how Ronnie and I would have visited all the islands together." Tamsin stood up and tightened the belt of her red sun-suit.

"I meant to tell you, Mum. I had a letter smuggled out from Sparks. He's very low in spirits but forgives me for my part in his downfall. He said he's in love with me . . . . "

"Like Ronnie did?" cut in Kate.

Tamsin bit her lip ruefully. "Yes, like Ronnie did."

They went to breakfast and afterwards found that once again they were to go ashore by launch.

"I can't make up my mind whether I prefer going by launch or tying up to the dock," said Tamsin. "It's sort of romantic going by launch but it's a bit inconvenient, having to wait your turn to go and then having to queue to get back on the ship. It's so much easier to walk on and off as you please." She gathered her bag and sunglasses. "Who are you going ashore with today, Mum?"

"No-one in particular," replied Kate.

"What! The famous *femme fatale* not having an escort? I'll have to see what I can do."

"No, please don't do me any more favours." Kate looked imploringly at her daughter as they walked along the deck. "I'm really looking forward to being on my own. I'm going to enjoy myself. After yesterday . . ."

Tamsin was all ears. "What happened yesterday?"

"It was most embarrassing." Kate put on her sunglasses. "Guy took me to a beach and Damon turned up, accompanied by that redhead, whom incidentally I've discovered is a very important passenger who goes by the name of the Honourable Esmeralda Fenshawe."

"No!" gasped Tamsin. "Lady La-de-da, eh? I hope you kept your end up."

"I don't know about keeping my end up," said Kate grimly, "but I managed to put Guy's nose out of joint. And that's the last thing I wanted to do."

"Oh, he'll survive." Tamsin laughed excitedly. "What about you and Damon?"

Before Kate could answer they noticed Damon and Guy standing on the platform outside the bridge. The latter called down to them as they prepared to disembark. "Have a nice day! Wish I could join you but two days ashore on the trot would be stretching the captain's generosity."

Damon's eyes took in Kate's tank-top and shorts. "That was a sneaky trick you played on me last night. Running out on me like that."

"Hey, what is all this?" demanded Guy suspiciously. "What happened last night?"

Kate ignored them both and quickened her step towards the steep steps going down the side of the ship.

"Hm! Nice little situation developing there," said Tamsin with a grin. "And you haven't answered my question. What about you and Damon?"

Kate blinked. "What? Oh, we sang a duet together, several in fact, on a karaoke machine."

"You? I don't believe it. Not my

mother who's always been so prim and proper."

"Yes," Kate said slowly. "Sometimes I don't recognise myself." She frowned suddenly. "Your father would be very upset if he could see me. All the things I've been doing on this ship! If you'd told me a week ago I'd be singing in public I'd have laughed in your face." She took the hand that a burly seaman offered and swung herself into the boat. "Oh Tamsin, my dear, I feel so guilty at times."

"Don't." Tamsin put her arm around Kate's shoulders. "Daddy wouldn't want you to go through life being miserable."

Kate looked thoughtful and murmured, almost to herself, "You know, I think perhaps Peter would expect me to be miserable."

"Mum! That's a terrible thing to say."

"Is it? Since I stepped aboard several things have become clear. I never thought I'd say this, but your father was rather narrow-minded." Kate glanced away from Tamsin's accusing eyes. "It sounds disloyal but it's true."

They arrived at the tiny dock and Tamsin went off with Harry.

Kate looked about her. Everything seemed to be in miniature. The shops and cafes were tiny and there were sweet little squares where the wrought-iron balconies were ablaze with geraniums.

She chose a cafe with a terrace overlooking the bay and ordered a floater coffee. She was leaning back in her chair with her eyes closed when she heard someone speak her name.

"Kate!" It was a woman's voice and she recognised it.

"All by yourself?" asked Esmeralda. "Mind if I join you?" And without waiting for an answer she dropped into a vacant chair.

"What do you want?" Kate was hard pressed to be civil.

"Do I have to want anything?"

"I reckon so." Kate surprised herself

with her blunt talk, but she didn't want to encourage the woman.

"All right," said the other. "I'll come straight to the point. Damon's mine!"

Kate sat bolt upright. For a moment she was unable to believe her ears. "What did you say?"

"You heard me."

"Yes, I heard you." She swivelled round in her chair to see Esmeralda more clearly. "I couldn't believe you said that."

"Well, it's best to be honest so we both know where we stand." Esmeralda met Kate's eyes boldly. "So as he's mine you won't need to waste your time on him."

A demon raised its head in Kate's brain. "Oh, what makes you so sure he's yours? I have't noticed him squiring you around."

"What about yesterday? He drove me to my aunt's."

"That was in the line of duty."

"Oh, was it?" Esmeralda sounded smug. "Don't you believe it. He could

173

have detailed the job to someone else."

"Well, I shared the middle watch with him last night." The moment the words were out Kate regretted them. She wasn't in competition with Esmeralda and it made her feel cheap to fight over Damon.

Esmeralda stared at Kate, her eyes hate-filled, her expression disbelieving. "I warn you, I've got connections. I could further his career. Besides being twenty years younger than you."

The bitch! thought Kate. No way was Esmeralda seventeen. She'd had enough of the woman. "Like I said, you're welcome to him."

"Do you mean that?"

"I most certainly do," said Kate getting up and leaving the cafe.

Outside in the warm air she shook her head in amazement. It was another first. She had been warned off a man.

6

MOTHER and daughter gazed out of the window as the ship travelled towards the small island of San Salute. It appeared round and very flat, rather like a dark-green upturned scallop shell floating on the turquoise sea. As they drew closer they observed clusters of wooden houses huddling together on pink beaches. They came to a narrow channel leading to a lagoon, and sailed in to tie up at the end of a wide floating dock.

"It's enchanting!" exclaimed Tamsin. "Just like Treasure Island."

Kate grinned suddenly. "Let's go ashore together today. Just the two of us."

"Good idea!" agreed Tamsin readily. "We'll give the lads the cold shoulder."

Another steel band greeted them with reggae music and the usual coffee stall had been set up at the end of the floating dock, with a reminder to be back on board by six o'clock. As they walked along the wooden planks Kate gazed into the pellucid water where she could see the ocean's coral floor and irridescent fish.

An Italian cruise ship and a French naval destroyer were berthed nearby and several luxury yachts were anchored in mid-lagoon. At the end of the dock, men were loading green bananas onto scores of inter-island boats the size of fishing smacks for transportation to one of the larger islands where they would be transferred to container ships.

San Salute was slightly larger than Cozummel and the main town was as commercialised as any other tourist place, but with a certain amount of history charmingly preserved. They wandered among terracotta buildings, past arched doorways and along narrow 'step alleys' leading to small squares where palm trees shaded tables set outside cafes and bars.

The inhabitants seemed a mixed bunch and most of them looked very poor. Time and again they were surrounded by children begging for money, and responded generously.

They took a bus tour around the island, driving through vast plantations of bananas which seemed to be the mainstay of the economy.

Kate was surprised to see that the bananas grew upwards. "I would have bet a hundred pounds they grew downwards," she laughed.

The sand on the beaches had a fine texture and the sea pounding on the thousands of conch shells had coloured it pink — the driver informed them in broken English.

"Isn't this the prettiest island you ever saw?" asked Tamsin after they had alighted and swum from an idyllic beach fringed with bougainvillea, oleander and hibiscus.

"Yes," agreed Kate, "But there is so much poverty here. It must be disquieting for the San Salutians to see people like us, squandering our money."

"Why is it the prettiest places are always the worst off?"

Back in the main square, the entertainments officer had arranged for the passengers to witness the famous San Salutian fire dance — a wild and often violent spectacle in which the dancers carried lighted torches. The music was provided by maracas, drums and guitars and the rhythm was a mixture of calypso and goombay. The costumes were exotic combining cotton and straw with fresh fruit and flowers.

Tamsin recorded everything with her video camera. "Another set for the honeymoon album," she quipped, and added acidly. "The only person missing is the groom. That rat Ronnie Kingsnorth."

When they eventually returned to the ship a large group of workers milled around the entrance to the dock and Kate sensed a feeling of unrest among them. Several of the banana boats were putting out from the shore and a dozen of them were anchored in the narrow channel leading to the open sea.

As they stepped onto the ship's deck a message was being relayed over the public address system. "Will all passengers kindly report to the Mainbrace Lounge at seven thirty when the captain will address you on a matter of some urgency".

"I wonder what's up," said Kate anxiously.

The message was repeated at regular intervals.

They joined the rest of the passengers in the lounge and listened to the buzz of nervous conversation. The fact that the ship had not sailed at seven o'clock appeared ominous.

Damon looked grave as he took the microphone. "Ladies and gentlemen, I'm afraid I have bad news. The local banana-boatmen have a dispute with their employers over pay and conditions. They've chained their boats together in the lagoon to form a blockade. They intend that no ship shall enter or leave the island until their demands have been met. I'm afraid we may be in for a long wait."

A thread of panic ran through the assembly and everyone started talking at once. Damon let them have their say for a moment then held up his hand for silence.

"I'm going ashore in a few moments to see if anything can be done to get us out of this predicament. We're not the only ship to be caught in this blockade. There's the Italian cruise ship and the French naval destroyer and all those luxury yachts. Representatives of them all have been invited to an informal meeting."

"How long will we be stuck here?" someone shouted. "I've got an important meeting the day after the cruise finishes."

Others joined in and started asking questions. Damon waited until they were quiet again. "At the moment you know as much as I do. I hope to have more information when I return."

He swiftly left the stage.

"Well, this is a turn up for the books," muttered Guy in Kate's ear. "I hate it when things differ from the norm. People are apt to panic and have heart attacks."

Presently the passengers, strangely quiet, lined the decks to watch the captain go ashore.

Kate studied his broad back, the immaculate white uniform, as he walked along the quay.

"Will he be in any danger?" she asked as a sudden anxiety assailed her. "Why does he have to go alone?"

"Those were the conditions stipulated." Guy watched her shrewdly. "Damon knows how to take care of himself."

"That wasn't the question."

"He'll be okay," Guy assured her. "He's armed. I saw him slip a revolver into his pocket before he left so don't you worry about that."

Kate gasped. "So there is some danger?"

Guy shrugged loosely. "These people are a wild, undisciplined lot. They're descended from Puritans and bucanneers — not a happy combination. There may be a few bully-boys trying to manipulate things and throw their weight about. Don't worry, this is all in a day's work to Damon. He can be very diplomatic when he likes. And if all else fails he'll have a trick or two up his sleeve. You'll see."

Dinner was over before the captain returned to the ship. He declined to answer any questions from the clamouring passengers and went directly to his office. A short time later they were all summoned to the Mainbrace Lounge again.

Damon's face appeared tired and haggard after two hours of talks and although he tried to put a brave front on, he seemed less confident than at the earlier meeting.

"I'm afraid the banana-boatmen

refuse to offer any concessions. We're doing all we can and I'll be going ashore again tomorrow." He forced a grin. "Well, you know what they say. Tomorrow's another day. I must ask you to remain on board in case we're permitted to leave at short notice."

He answered a further barrage of questions which, Kate reflected, left no-one any the wiser.

The entertainments officer took the microphone and announced, with a frozen smile, that there would be a special party with fun and games at midnight on Dolphin Deck.

Damon took advantage of this diversion to quit the stage and make for the door. Kate was sitting at the back near the aisle and as he drew level with her chair, he held out his hand. She grasped it without thinking, disregarding the little warning voice in her brain, and allowed him to steer her outside.

Damon tucked Kate's arm through his and continued walking fast so that she had to stretch her legs to keep pace with him. He stopped in the heavy shadow of a funnel.

It was late evening now and the stars twinkled above them like diamonds on a bed of black velvet. Any other time, Kate would have been moved by the beauty of the night.

"What a mess!" Damon threw his cap onto a nearby deckchair and Kate's heart went out to him as she watched him in the gloom.

"Those talks were a shambles." He placed one foot on the bottom rung of the rail and leaned his elbows on the top.

She sensed an affinity between them that was almost tangible. There were dozens of questions she wanted to ask, but she held her tongue.

"Everyone was talking at once," he said bitterly. "It was a case of arrogance and ignorance meeting head on and commonsense getting lost in the cross-fire. It's only the few foreign ships that are concerned. The rest of the

crafts belong to the island community."
He pursed his lips thoughtfully for a
moment. "The irony is I can see
the boatmen have a grievance and
I'm inclined to agree with them. The
employers are living in the past in
their crumbling mansions and sinking
deeper in debt. No wonder they can't
pay the workers a decent wage. Their
equipment is archaic — machetes for
the harvesting of the crop and donkey
carts to transport the bananas to the
dock. They should have their own
container ships instead of ferrying the
crop to other islands and handing
them a rake-off of the profits. A wage
increase won't help the situation either,
it'll just bankrupt the place."

Kate studied the animated expressions
darting across his face as his concern
for the islanders transmitted itself to
her.

He laughed wryly. "All that aside,
I have a deadline to meet and an
eighty-thousand pound ship to worry
about, to say nothing of five hundred

crew and eight hundred passengers."
His eyes bored into her. "One of them
very special indeed."

She felt his warm breath fanning
her cheek and grew flustered suddenly.
"You must be busy . . . "

He straightened from the rail and
loosely took her chin in his free hand.

She trembled violently.

"Cold, Kate?" he asked, "or scared?
Are you frightened of this blockade
business?"

"No, I don't think so."

"Scared of me then?"

"No." She hesitated. "Scared for you.
I was anxious when you went ashore.
Guy said there could be trouble and
when he said you were armed . . . "

"Guy talks too much." Damon
dropped his head to plant a swift
kiss on her lips sending a thrill of
delight thudding down her spine.

"Please . . . someone will see us . . . "

"No, we're out of sight of prying eyes.
Besides," he reasoned, "They're too
busy sorting out their affairs, sending

cables to their families and business associates, arranging for more funds to be made available."

"I thought you had a crisis on your hands," she protested weakly.

"Which crisis are you referring to?" he asked playfully. "The blockade or Mrs Kate Ashley?"

She didn't know how to answer, but was spared having to try because at that moment the loudspeaker beside them blared out: "Will Captain Penrose please contact the radio room immediately for an urgent message."

Damon shrugged. "That'll be the other crisis. It's probably London. They're lobbying foreign ministers. Wish me luck, Kate!"

"Good luck!"

"Don't I get a good-luck kiss?"

She hung her head, shy all of a sudden. This was all getting too much for her.

He swept her into his arms and planted a noisy kiss on her lips. She felt a surge of desire slice through her like a knife through butter.

She arrived back in the cabin in a state of shock feeling as if she'd been tossed in a terrible storm which had torn her senses to shreads and left her heart exposed to the elements.

"I'm all mixed up over Damon," she told Tamsin. "And now we're stuck in this lagoon for goodness knows how long. I can't stand it any more. All I want to do is go home and get on with my life. Oh, I wish we'd never come on this cruise."

"Amen to that," agreed Tamsin.

A crisis brought out the best in people, Kate reflected, as she sat in a deckchair by the pool helping to keep the little children amused. Everyone was being so friendly towards each other. They were like one big happy family. And Damon was their father figure.

Kate wrapped her arms closer about a small girl who had fallen asleep on her lap and pondered the enigma that was Damon Penrose. Her feelings for him were all physical, she knew, and she would get over it. He was the last man on earth for her. Imagine living with someone like that! It would be like being constantly on a roller-coaster. The sooner she got back to Maidstone and her sane dull existence the better. And in the short term she must keep away from him.

She wished she could banish him from her mind, but her thoughts gravitated to him like pins to a magnet. Just as she wondered if the sun had addled her brain, the cause of her heart-searching walked along the deck and stopped before her.

Damon's eyes raked her swimsuit and bare limbs, then lifted lazily to her face, wreaking havoc to her resolve to stay away from him. He smiled down at the sleeping child. "It suits you, Kate."

He crouched down beside the deckchair and gently smoothed the little girl's golden hair. "I'm going ashore again in a few moments to see if I can persuade them to let us go."

"Oh!" Kate's anxiety made her throat contract. "Take care, Damon."

The child stirred and he stood up.

"Good luck!" she said.

His lips twitched. "You can give me the 'good luck' kiss when I return."

"Just see you do return."

He gazed into her anxious blue eyes. "I don't know what Guy's been saying, but he had no right to frighten you. There's no danger, believe me, Kate."

She remained unconvinced. He wouldn't be likely to tell her in any case. "If you say so."

Later Kate joined the rest of the passengers lining the decks to watch Damon go ashore again. She felt a tight knot of apprehension in her stomach as she gazed at his tall figure striding away. Despite his assurances, he could be walking into all kinds of trouble. Guy had already made it clear that the San Salutians were an excitable race. Now they were incensed and fighting for their livelihood . . .

A hush fell over the watchers as Damon disappeared from view.

All at once the silence was shattered by what sounded like rifle shots!

Kate clutched the rail as a cold shaft of terror tore through her. She wanted to run the length of the floating dock, but managed somehow to restrain the impulse.

The people around her were stunned with shock then a woman screamed. A wave of hysteria swept through them like wildfire and they began speculating noisily as to what could have happened.

The loudspeakers crackled and a voice said, "Please stay calm. We are in contact with Captain Penrose by walkie-talkie and there is no cause for alarm. Those shots were fired by some over-excited youths with air rifles. No-one was harmed and they've been arrested."

A sigh of relief rippled through the assembly, but Kate's vivid imagination was working overtime. What if those bully-boys decided to get tough? There could be ugly scenes — and Damon would be right in the thick of it. She pictured him lying wounded . . . dead . . . a red stain spreading over that immaculate uniform.

The images shaping themselves in her mind gradually faded and she mentally took herself in hand. She was being morbid and melodramatic. What she needed was something to keep her occupied, she decided.

What could she do to while away the time, she wondered, going towards her cabin. Some washing? Read a book?

She washed a few things through but that only took fifteen minutes. So, as Damon still had not returned, she might as well get a book, and she took the lift to the library in the bowels of the ship.

Kate trailed her fingertips along the spines of the books, scanning the titles with unseeing eyes. He had been gone over an hour.

Focusing on the shelves, she hooked out an 'Agatha Christie' and dashed out. She walked straight into Guy, looking every inch a doctor in his white coat with a stethoscope round his neck.

He steadied her with a firm hand. "You look terrible, Kate. What have you been doing to yourself? Here, come into the sick-bay and take the weight off your feet." As he led her through a pair of perspex doors her nostrils were assaulted by the smell of antiseptics.

They passed through a white-walled corridor where the pretty young nurse was sterilising instruments. Beyond her Kate glimpsed a small operating theatre and a six-bed ward, empty she was pleased to note. She had no idea the ship was so well equipped.

"Come into my office." Guy threw open a door and stood back for her to enter the small windowless room furnished with several filing cabinets, a desk and some chairs.

"What's up, Kate?" he asked pushing her gently into an armchair. "All this waiting getting you down?" He took the chair behind the desk. "You don't have to worry about Damon. He'll be perfectly all right."

Oh dear she thought, was it so obvious?

"But he's been gone for so long."

"Has he?" Guy glanced at his watch. "I'm out of touch down here. We don't have loudspeakers in the sick-bay. It disturbs the patients." He drummed his fingers on the desk. "Damon has a lot of trouble. The weather report he received this morning indicated a storm, force eleven, heading this way."

The breath caught painfully in Kate's throat. "Oh no!"

"That's classified information by the way," said Guy. "Damon doesn't want a panic on his hands."

She nodded.

"The Skipper has to work fast now so he'll be pulling out all the stops. It's imperative that we leave as soon as possible."

"But we're in a lagoon. Surely we're

in the best place to shelter from a storm."

"No, we're not!" he declared grimly. "A man-made harbour is the best place to shelter from a storm. But this lagoon is nature-made. And it faces the wrong way. The island is too flat to offer any protection to us. We'll get the full brunt if we remain here."

"Can't the passengers be boarded out on shore?"

"There isn't enough accommodation on the island to put up eight hundred passengers, plus a similar number from the Italian cruise ship. Even if there were, Damon has the ship itself to think of. It's worth a king's ransom."

"Poor Damon," said Kate. "He certainly has a lot to worry about. Why doesn't the Company send someone from London to sort things out? It seems so unfair."

"They prefer to leave this sort of thing to the man on the spot." He smiled gently. "Don't worry, Damon's an old hand at this sort of thing."

The pretty nurse popped her head round the door to say Guy was needed in surgery.

"Back in a tick," he said, rising. "Don't go away."

After he had left Kate got up restlessly and went to the water cooler in the corner. She was gulping down a cupful of the refreshing liquid when she heard someone come through the perspex doors.

"Guy, where are you?"

Kate's heart seemed to miss a beat as she recognised Damon's deep resonant voice. He was safe!

He walked into the office and saw her standing there. "Kate!" he exclaimed.

Tears of relief stung her eyes. She dropped the empty plastic cup and ran to throw her arms around his neck and pull his head down till his lips touched hers.

His hands met behind her back and he studied her misted lashes. "What brought that on?"

She withdrew her arms from his neck

and brought them to rest against his chest. "I'm so thankful you're back. I didn't know . . . They don't have loudspeakers in the sick bay." She noticed the little stress lines besides his mouth and the fatigue ringing his eyes. "Did you solve anything?"

"It's difficult to say. I piled it on about the value of the ship and the effect of the . . . " He stopped abruptly.

"I know about the storm," she said quickly.

"Guy told you, I suppose." He sighed resignedly. "I must have a serious word with Guy. And I must ask that you don't let that information go any further."

"Of course. I won't say a word."

"I've managed to convince both sides of the dispute that they need a mediator — and offered myself," he went on gravely. "The employers must get off their backsides and move into the twentieth century. If they don't acquire better boats and equipment and start improving conditions they'll go bankrupt and the island will be finished. On the other hand, the workers must be made to understand the importance of hard graft and pride in their efforts."

He still had his arms around her and she liked it. "I'm going to cable the company in a moment to suggest we pour financial support into the island until they begin to show a profit. I can't see them objecting, after all San Salute is one of our ports of call and we'd like to see it prosper. There's a whole lot of potential here. If I can get all sides to see the advantages we'll be halfway there. The trouble is that the bully-boys appear to be running the dispute and it suits their nefarious purposes to ruin the economy in order to pick up the pieces at rock bottom prices. Both sides appear to be scared of them. Anyway, they're all thinking it over now, so we'll wait and see." His lips slanted and there was a definite a gleam in his sea-green eyes. "I think I'll collect that 'good luck' kiss now."

She wriggled selfconsciously, still

trapped in his arms. "You've just had it."

"No, that was a 'welcome back' kiss." His eyes were as compelling as the ocean itself. "I'm waiting, Kate."

She lifted her mouth, intending to give him a peck on the cheek, but he gathered her to him more closely and his lips met hers with a primitive force which left her dazed and weak. His hands, their warmth tangible through her thin crystal-pleated dress, dispersed a river of flame down her spine.

After the emotion-dredged events of the morning, this assault on her nerves was more than she could handle. She shuddered and made a feeble effort to free herself from the web of yearning he so skilfully spun, but it was too late. Her very soul seemed to contain a furnace which sent slivers of passion through her veins like molten wax.

"I could stay here all day." His voice was curiously gentle as he let her go. "But, just in case things don't go as I hope, I have to plan my strategy."

"S . . . strategy?"

He laid his finger against the side of his nose. "Mum's the word, Kate."

He stepped away from her then stopped as if remembering something and fished in his breast pocket to produce a sapphire-blue square of lace. It was as fine as gossamer and crisscrossed with gold thread. "I almost forgot. An old lady was selling scarves from the end of the dock. I thought this colour would match your eyes." He held it up to check then hooked it round her neck, pulled her towards him by the ends and kissed the tip of her nose.

Kate was choking with emotion as she stammered her thanks, amazed that with all his worries he still had time to think about the colour of her eyes.

He went outside and she heard him in the corridor, calling out to Guy. "Where are you hiding, for Pete's sake? This is important."

Kate was consumed by conflicting thoughts as she returned to her cabin.

It was no good beating about the bush any longer. She was in love with him! The acceptance of the truth, pure, simple and irrefutable, sent her heart palpitating and her nails digging painfully into her palms. It must be the effect of the cruise and the trauma of the blockade and, God only knew, it had to be temporary! But it was a fact nevertheless. She'd known him just eight days and gone overboard! She'd fallen for a tall, dark stranger who could only mean trouble. For whatever happened, there was no future in it. She must hold on to her sanity until they finished the cruise . . . whenever that would be. Any weakening now would precipitate disaster. He was a rover. Not the kind to fall.

She wondered how long she had loved him, recalling the electric current in his handshake that first night in the officers' mess. Or was it earlier than that? The minute she had come aboard and his gaze had so disturbed her? For the chemistry which had sparked between them then could no longer be denied.

When Tamsin came in she found her mother lying on the bed staring at the ceiling.

"What's up?" she asked, flinging the wardrobe door wide and rifling through the hangers. "You look strange."

"You were right."

"In what way?" Tamsin selected a turquoise evening gown with sequins smothering the bodice.

"When you said I was a woman overboard."

Tamsin didn't realise the significance of Kate's remark at once. When it dawned she turned her big blue eyes on her. "I'm wondering if I did the right thing inviting you on this cruise with me. You're so innocent and vulnerable you could get hurt. Then I'll be to blame."

"Whatever happens, I shan't blame you," said Kate, "And stop saying I'm naive. I've been a married woman."

"Yes, a very sheltered one."

★ ★ ★

Watching the captain go ashore seemed to have become part of the routine, thought Kate, leaning on the rail until he was swallowed up in a little knot of people at the far end of the floating dock. The passengers were not so apprehensive now. Just after lunch a delegation of San Salutians had come aboard and it was generally understood that they had accepted Damon's offer to mediate in their dispute.

However this time it seemed he had gone for good and, as day turned into night, most of them drifted away to crowd the ship's bars and lounges.

Kate remained on deck until she saw Damon return, just after ten. It was only then her empty stomach reminded her she had missed dinner and she wandered down to one of the snack-bars to get herself a sandwich and a cup of tea. She was depositing her paper napkin in the disposal bag when the announcement of yet another meeting in the Mainbrace Lounge was broadcast. Did it mean more trouble?

There was an air of grim determination about Damon as he mounted the stage and it seemed to Kate that something momentous was afoot.

In clear concise language Damon told his hushed, attentive audience that after several hours of negotiating the talks had broken down.

Kate heard the sighs of disappointment all around her and her shoulders slumped dejectedly.

Damon explained that everything had appeared to be going extremely well and he'd had the islanders eating out of his hand. He'd pointed out the advantages of modern equipment and organisation and offered financial backing which had been provisionally accepted. The workers had been prepared to remove the blockade . . . then it had happened. The heavies had moved in and closed the meeting, refusing point black to allow any further discussion.

Damon jutted his jaw in a resolute

manner. "That's it then, ladies and gentlemen. I refuse to be dictated to by a bunch of thugs. The time for talking is past. Now it's time for action. We're leaving!"

7

THE atmosphere in the lounge was tense as they waited, bemused, for the captain to continue.

He paused dramatically looking round at the passengers. At last he said, "I've decided to take the law into my own hands to get us out of this situation. In precisely thirty minutes' time the s.s Jamestown Pearl will make an attempt to escape from the blockade."

A babble of excited chatter greeted this announcement, but he held up his hand for silence. Everyone stopped talking and seemed to hold their breath.

"A short time ago," Damon went on, "four of the crew — an experienced officer and three frogmen — rowed the inflatable dinghy to the blockade of boats. I have just received the message over the walkie-talkie that they are in position. We had already ascertained that there was only one man on duty at the blockade, stationed in the middle boat. He has been dealt with as gently as possible."

A ripple of laughter broke out, relieving some of the tension in the lounge.

"The frogmen will cut the four middle boats from the blockade and weigh the anchors," Damon explained. "At eleven-thirty precisely they will start the engine of one boat and tow the other three out of the channel, aided by a fresh wind and an ebb tide. The boats will be anchored just outside the lagoon. The frogmen will have marked what remains of the blockade with lights to guide us through. The dinghy will make for the open sea and if we are successful we will pick them up later."

Kate clasped Tamsin's hand as a bubble of excitement threatened to choke her and her admiration for

Damon's stategy knew no bounds.

"There's no moon tonight and the sky is overcast," he said. "We'll carry on as normal showing all our deck lights and with our dance orchestras making plenty of noise. A few minutes before we make the run all lights will be doused, including cabin and navigational lights, and silence will be observed. That will include you." His eyes swept earnestly over the gathering. "It's now or never! The first ship to beat the blockade will be the last. If the Italian cruise ship or French destroyer try it before us, the bullies will be more vigilant and we'll stand no chance. Tomorrow could be too late."

"What if the others are already planning making a run for it tonight?" asked someone.

"We'll all collide," quipped another.

Damon joined in the laughter which ensued. "I'm confident they're not planning anything tonight because they've allowed their passengers and crews ashore to sample the nightlife of the San Salute." He paused. "If anyone wishes to be excluded from this dash for freedom, for health reasons or whatever, please report to the purser's office at once. Members of the crew are standing by to take you ashore in the launch."

Nobody moved.

Damon's shoulders rose and fell expressively. "I must stress this is entirely my own decision and has nothing to do with the company. So you know who to blame if we don't make it. One word of warning. If the bully-boys get wind of what we're doing they may try to stop us — by sailing out in force so that we're obliged to halt for fear of running them down. If I have to jam the brakes on hard it might be unpleasant. I don't want people falling over in the dark, so stay in your cabins, lie on your beds — and pray!"

He was playing down the danger, thought Kate, but she recalled his urgent concern to speak with Guy that morning. Was it to make sure the sick-bay was ready to cope with any casualties that may result from this particular escapade? It had to be. Her vivid imagination ran riot. They could be rammed by the bully boys' boats . . . boarded . . . fired upon . . . They could be killed!

* * *

Kate and Tamsin lay on their beds staring out of the window at the still water in which was reflected the blazing lights of the shore establishments. The ship was unusually quiet and the sounds from the town carried over the lagoon with eerie clarity.

Their cabin lights had gone out a few moments earlier and they were aware that the bid for freedom was about to begin.

There came a knock on the door and Guy, carrying a torch, popped his head round. "Mind if I join you?"

He felt his way to an armchair and sat down. "Everything's quiet in the sick-bay. I've dished out a few sedatives to the older generation, but everyone else seems to be taking things calmly. Damon has that effect. I'll have to return in a moment, but thought I'd share this historic occasion with you."

They felt a sudden throb as the engines burst into life and Tamsin said, "I'm so excited, my heart is simply hammering."

"I suppose Damon had to take that into account," mused Kate, thinking again of his anxiety to see Guy that morning, "People having coronaries and the like."

"Yes, who'd be captain?" asked Guy.

The three of them gazed out as the lights of San Salute appeared to sweep past with the gathering speed of the ship. Soon they saw a dark mass which could only be the depleted blockade, sporting a solitary red light.

Everything seemed to be going to plan.

Kate felt the adrenalin feeding her bloodstream and whispered, "Damon must have nerves of steel."

"That's why he's captain," rejoined Guy.

They were startled by signs of activity on the shore — the lights of cars and torches moving around. Several boats were speeding towards them. Then a searchlight cast its beam over the ship and Kate was forced to close her eyes against the concentrated brightness. "They've seen what we're doing," she groaned as a spasm of disappointment trembled through her. "They're going to stop us. So near and yet so far. Oh how disappointing."

"They haven't stopped us yet," Guy pointed out. "If Damon can squeeze a bit more speed out of her . . . "

Two boats came alongside and flashed a signal lamp.

"They're ordering us to stop," explained Guy. "Damon will take no notice."

Kate was sitting on the edge of her bed and her stomach was twisted into a tight knot of tension. "But if they get in front of us . . . "

"They're too late," said Guy excitedly. "We're through."

The ship's hooter began to sound triumphantly, three short blasts followed by one long one.

"V for victory," explained Guy as the lights came on in the cabin. He jumped from his chair, hauled Kate from the bed to waltz round the room with her, then kissed her full on the lips. "My God, he's done it!"

Every bell and hooter on the ship began to sound in a great cacophony of noise and they heard people outside in the passageway chanting, "We want the captain, we want the captain!"

Kate and Tamsin joined in the general stampede making for the bridge. Eventually Damon stepped out onto the platform and the passengers sang "For He's a Jolly Good Fellow".

Half a dozen of the men stormed the platform and Damon was borne shoulder-high along the deck. The blacked-up frogmen had arrived on

213

board now and were given the same treatment.

Damon was set down on the deck and people surged round eager to shake his hand.

He sent for a loudhailer and finally managed to restore order. "Ladies and gentlemen, I'm flattered by your appreciation, but the San Salutians are simple people and it wasn't too difficult to get the better of them. Frankly they couldn't run a kids' tea party, let alone a blockade. Anyone could have handled it . . ."

He was too modest and loud cries of protest drowned his words.

He continued, "I want to thank you all for keeping your heads and doing exactly as I asked. I'm proud of you all. There was no panic and no casualties." He grinned suddenly. "Apart from one gentleman who, I understand, stumbled into the wrong cabin in the dark and received a black eye."

Hoots of laughter greeted his joke.

His eyes began eagerly scanning the crowd before him. "There's a warning of a storm in this area, but we'll be miles away by the time it arrives. We've lost a day while we've been stuck here so we'll have to miss out on the planned visit to Cat Island. We'll now make straight for Miami. The entertainments officer tells me he has plenty of good things in store for you, including the fancy dress ball tomorrow . . . I mean tonight." His eyes found Kate's at last and stayed there. "I'll see you there."

"Might as well turn in, I'm so tired," said Tamsin. "I'm pleased to have been part of it all. We'll be able to dine out on the blockade for ages." She yawned. "It's been quite a day."

Yes, thought Kate. It wasn't every day she escaped from the confines of a physical blockade only to find herself in the throes of an emotional one. She wondered how she was going to handle it. She wasn't used to hiding her feelings, she'd had no need. But she had already decided nothing good could come from Damon knowing how she felt. She only hoped she was up to keeping the secret.

★ ★ ★

"Are we news!" exclaimed Nelson, coming in with the early morning coffee. "Our captain's picture is spashed all over the front page of every newspaper in the world. I told you he was one of the best."

"Will he receive another medal?" asked Tamsin, lolling in the armchair.

"I shouldn't be at all suprised." Nelson savoured the prospect as he placed the daily news sheets on the table. "They're calling him 'the hero of San Salute'. The man's a genius. Our escape called the bully-boys' bluff and they've crawled away with their tails between their legs. The island's all set to solve its problems and prosper — thanks to the captain."

"Nelson was right," observed Tamsin

later as they stood on deck and watched a couple of press helicopters circling the ship prior to landing on the deck.

They interviewed the captain and the frogmen and took lots of photographs of the ship as well as some of the passengers. Everyone was keen to record their opinion.

After the choppers had departed a magnificent steam yacht came alongside the gangway steps. It was tall and sleek and glided over the water in a graceful curve. The passengers raced to the side to photograph it.

As it drew level with the steps a man leapt over and began the ascent while the yacht made a graceful turn and sped away.

The newcomer was a tall, slim young man with clean-cut handsome features and nutmeg-brown hair and moustache. He was impeccably dressed in a beige linen suit and white shirt and carried a small travel bag.

"Ronnie Kingsworth!" exclaimed Kate. "Whatever is he doing here?"

She studied her daughter's ashen face. "Steady on, Tammy, you look ready to faint."

"Ronnie!" whispered Tamsin, a dreamy expression clouding her china blue eyes. "He's come for me."

Ronnie had reached the deck and stood looking uncertainly about him. Then he caught sight of Tamsin and grinned sheepishly.

She gave a great cry of joy and rushed into his outstretched arms. For long moments they kissed and embraced, then Tamsin took his hand and led him towards Kate.

Kate eyed him suspiciously. "Hello, Ronnie. Aren't you a little late? The honeymoon was due to begin a week ago."

He had the grace to look ashamed. "I know! You have every right to be angry with me, Kate, I've been all kinds of a fool."

Tamsin was clinging possessively to his arm. "Don't be cross, Mum. Ronnie admits he was in the wrong. He loves me and wants to marry me."

"Where have I heard that before?" asked Kate dryly.

"Aw, come on, Kate." Ronnie's cultured drawl contained an apologetic tone. "I'm sorry for the way I behaved and I want to make amends." He squeezed Tamsin's hand and gazed adoringly into her face. "Can you ever forgive me, darling. I don't know what came over me. Guess I was plain scared by all the preparations. When I read about the blockade I was desperately worried for you, my darling. I suddenly realised I can't live without you." He kissed her forehead. "I flew down to Miami, took a small plane to the Bahamian islands then rented that splendid yacht and radioed the ship for permission to board."

"You certainly know how to do things in style," said Tamsin, her eyes aglow with admiration.

Kate let out an exasperated sigh. "I don't want to sound like a wet blanket, Ronnie, but Tamsin has been very unhappy."

"Has she?" He cuddled the girl more tightly. "My love, I've behaved badly, but I'll make it up to you, you'll see." He reached into the inner pocket of his jacket and waved a slip of paper. "I've brought the marriage licence with me. Captains can't marry people any more but I understand there's a chaplain on board, so there's no reason why we shouldn't get married straight away — today — if . . . if you agree."

"Oh Ronnie!" said Tamsin, her eyes shining like precious jewels . . . "Yes!"

Kate looked from one to the other of them and a slow smile spread over her features. She had known all along that Ronnie and Tamsin were made for each other. She was thankful that the affair was to have a happy ending after all. "Good luck!" she said, "I wish you all the happiness in the world."

Tamsin and Ronnie both kissed her cheek and went away to make their plans.

The wedding took place that afternoon in the tiny chapel on Savoy Deck. Tamsin, attired in a simple white dress and wearing one orchid which Ronnie had purchased from the ship's shop, looked positively radiant.

The couple had asked Kate and the captain to be witnesses to the marriage.

As Kate handed Damon the gold pen and watched as, with a bold sweep, he signed his name beneath hers, she was struck by the shattering realization that their names were together on a marriage certificate. Her thoughts took wing. Supposing it had been their wedding. It would mean the end of her freedom and her well-ordered life. It would mean constant waiting, wondering if he were alive or dead — or with another woman. It would mean being dominated by his forceful personality.

She trembled violently. What kind of insanity was this? She had no intention of marrying him — even in the remote likelihood that he would ask her. She accepted that she loved him, but knowing the futility of it all, had convinced herself that it was a transitory derangement on her part. She would get over it once she returned to the real world — please God!

A wedding breakfast had been prepared at very short notice and most of the passengers joined in the feast. Even a cake had been provided, a magnificent three-tiered creation with the tradional bridal figures on top.

"We have plenty of shipboard weddings and we always keep something in reserve," explained Damon. "People seem keen to leap into matrimony on a cruise. I only hope they don't live to regret it."

Dancing followed on the boat deck and Kate danced mostly with Guy. She wondered if she would get the chance to dance with Damon but he was busy in his office. Then just as the party was breaking up he appeared by her side.

"May I have the last dance?"

She had promised Guy the last dance and felt a bit mean going into Damon's arms. Over Damon's shoulder she saw Guy watching her with an expression of exasperation on his face.

"I shall have to move out of the cabin," she murmured as she and Damon danced a very stylish foxtrot. "I suppose I'll have to see the purser and see what he's got vacant. Wouldn't it be awful if he hasn't got anything. I'll have to sleep in one of the lifeboats like a stowaway."

"I've already made arrangements for you to move into one of the spare stateroom suites on the boat deck," said Damon.

"Oh but I couldn't . . . "

"No buts. There will be no extra charge. The accommodation comes with my compliments." He placed his hand in the small of her back. "So if you'd like to come along now, your steward is ready to effect the changeover."

Kate saw that it was a *fait accompli*

and accepted graciously.

She went to the cabin she had shared with Tamsin to supervise Nelson over the packing and was taking a last look round when Damon filled the doorway.

"Everything under control?" he asked.

"Yes thanks," replied Kate. "It's good of you to go to all this trouble on my account."

"Not at all."

"I'd be quite happy to move into an ordinary cabin."

"Why should you when we have a stateroom suite available?"

They followed Nelson as he pushed the trunk and cases on a trolley along the deck.

The staterooms were spacious, a sitting room and a bedroom, lavishly furnished in contemporary style with tubular steel chairs, dralon-covered armchairs, shag-pile carpeting, lots of Swedish glass, Picasso reproductions and a king-sized bed.

As they entered the sitting-room Mac

arrived with a tray of tea and biscuits which he set on one of the occasional tables.

"Oh, that's good of you Mac," said Kate. "I know you make a lovely cup of tea."

"Captain's orders, Ma'am." He eyed Damon slyly. "I brought just the one cup sir, knowing how busy you are and that you won't be stopping."

Damon jerked his head round and threw the man a stony glance. "You're doing a grand job, Mac," he said sarcastically.

"Oh aye sir. You can rely on me to keep my head under all circumstances . . ."

"If you want to keep your job," Damon interrupted him, "You'd better get the hell out of here."

Kate was confused by all the subtle undertones flowing between them.

Mac looked artfully from Damon to Kate then beat a hasty retreat.

Damon turned to the other steward who had deposited Kate's trunk in the middle of the bedroom and was awaiting further instructions. "You'll still look after Mrs Ashley, Nelson."

Kate marvelled on how he managed to remember the names of every member of crew.

Nelson grinned at Kate. "It'll be a pleasure, sir."

After the steward had left, Damon hung about in the doorway, seemingly loath to leave. "All right now? Have you everything you want?"

"Yes thanks," she replied impatiently, wanting him to go, wanting him to stay, finding it impossible to ignore the unnerving effect his presence was having on her. "Just as long as you understand these are my staterooms." Her cheeks flared. "I mean, just because they're *gratis*, I don't expect you to come waltzing in every time the fancy takes you . . . " She broke off with embarrassment, knowing that even as she spoke she wanted him to touch her.

He laughed easily. "These are your

staterooms, Kate. As to the rest — are you sure you don't want me waltzing in every time the fancy takes me?"

She stared at him and sighed eloquently. "You're impossible!"

He gripped her uplifted chin in one strong hand and planted a swift hard kiss on her lips, assuaging for the moment her yearning for his touch. "Kate! I'm not the one who's impossible." He turned to go. "But we'll argue that one later — when the fancy takes me."

He swivelled on his heel and stepped smartly over the threshold. "See you at the Fancy Dress Ball." He glanced at his watch. "In four hours' time."

Kate was enjoying her second cup of tea and thinking about getting to work on the unpacking, when her eyes fell on the gold braided cap lying on one of the armchairs. She frowned. Any moment now Damon would be missing that and have an excuse for coming back, unsettling her again. He may even have left it on purpose.

She picked it up and made her way along the deck to his office, hoping he would not be there and she would be able to leave it.

She nodded to the seamen in their outer office then 'knocked and entered' to find the main office deserted.

She was placing the cap on the desk when she heard voices coming from the open door leading to Damon's living quarters.

"Be careful sir, this one's different." It was Mac's rich Scottish accent.

"I'm aware of that, Mac." Damon sounded impatient.

There came the sound of a drawer being banged shut then Mac's voice again. "It could get serious."

"I know what I'm doing!"

"Oh aye. Famous last words, sir."

Kate knew instinctively they were talking about her and was rooted to the spot.

"It would be a pity to see a good man go under," Mac persisted.

"If all you can do is cluck like an

old hen, shut up and get out!"

"You could be playing with fire, sir."

"Get out!"

"All right, but don't come crying to me when you get your fingers burned. Sir!"

Kate heard tea-cups being placed noisily on a tray and pictured Mac's craggy features set in a stubborn line.

She fled before she was discovered eavesdropping and returned to her staterooms, her mind in a turmoil.

The words she had overheard sent shivers of anticipation coursing through her. She was different! It could get serious!

She controlled her quaking limbs and went to the entertainments office to select her fancy dress for the evening's ball. She chose a Brazilian outfit, a long red tiered dress with inserts of black lace and a daringly-low neckline.

Later as she affixed the 'Carmen Miranda' turban loaded with exotic fruit, made of lightweight plastic, she wondered what had made her pick something so sensual and evocative. She twirled about before the mirror watching the skirt float around her legs and knew she had dressed with one man in mind.

The ball was a noisy colourful event. Kate shared a table with Guy who was dressed as Henry Morgan, the pirate — complete with a stuffed parrot on his shoulder — and the Youngs, who had come as Laurel and Hardy. Tamsin and Ronnie were nowhere to be seen.

Harry Brown, disguised as a clown, was propping up the bar looking sorry for himself and getting quietly legless. Poor Harry, thought Kate sadly. He had been good for Tamsin, taking her ashore, gazing at her so fondly, helping her forget her heartache. He saw Kate watching him and raised his glass self-mockingly.

Kate was much in demand for the dancing, mainly with Guy, and the ball was well under way before Damon came to ask her to join him on the floor.

He appeared positively dashing in his dress uniform, the short black jacket decorated with medal ribbons and a gold lanyard.

"No fancy dress?" she enquired as they mingled with the dancers for a modern waltz.

"I might get called to the bridge." He laughed, executing a stylish reverse turn. "It wouldn't do for me to arrive in a gorilla suit." He glanced down at her outfit. "Very nice."

"Thank you."

The dance ended and he escorted her back to her table. Moments later she saw him dancing with Esmeralda who looked stunning, as usual, in a clinging Grecian gown. And he was laughing and whispering with her in the same intimate manner.

Jealousy raged through Kate like a forest fire, enflaming her nerves and making her cheeks flare. Trembling, she made her excuses to Guy and the Youngs.

"Are you okay?" Guy watched her

closely. "Is there something I can do?"

"No, please don't trouble. I've got a headache that's all."

He glanced to where Damon and the redhead were performing an elegant bossa nova. "Another?"

"Yes!" She almost ran to her staterooms.

She removed her head-dress then went into the bedroom and without turning on the light, sat in the armchair listlessly staring out at the moonless sky. Had she been mistaken about the conversation she had overheard between Damon and his steward? Perhaps they'd been talking about someone else. Esmeralda? No, thought Kate, they were talking about me! Then why hadn't Damon been more attentive? She sighed as she put on her pyjamas. Nothing made sense any more.

She put on the bedlight and climbed into bed meaning to get to grips with the Agatha Christie novel. But she couldn't concentrate. Damon was on her mind. Oh why was she beating about the bush? She wanted him to come to her, had thought he would.

Her wayward thoughts filled her with excitement. How she had changed! She was no longer the naive girl Peter had married. In some way she felt ashamed. And guilty. She had never felt this way about her husband, hadn't really known what true love was. She hadn't thought about him for days, and never would again — not in that same special way. For her world had changed irrevocably and she could no longer claim comfort from his memory. This emotion that she was experiencing now was the real thing, she was sure — because it hurt so. It had always puzzled her when people spoke about the pain of love. Now she understood.

There was still time for him to come!

She must have dozed off for she was woken later by a slight sound from the other room.

She observed a streak of light

under the door and a glance at the illuminated wall-clock told her it was one-thirty. She slid silently out of bed and, opening the door, asked sleepily, "Who's there?"

"I'm sorry if I disturbed you," said Damon. "I've misplaced a memo and wondered if I dropped it here this afternoon."

She was fully awake now and on her guard. "Oh really?" she asked dryly, now that he was here wishing him gone, contrary as ever. "My door was locked."

"All doors open to the captain."

"I thought you promised not to wander in here."

"I made no promises." His eye explored her figure in the lemon silk pyjamas as she stood framed in the doorway.

"Did you really misplace a memo?"

He flung his cap onto a chair and crossed the room. "What do you think?"

"Please . . . go away," she wavered.

"I . . . don't want you here."

"I don't believe you, Kate." He ran his fingers down her cheek and into the hollow beside her lips, watching them tremble despite her efforts to keep them still. "The only thing that will make me go away now is the phone ringing with the message that the ship is sinking."

"So you've told everyone where you are? Thanks."

"No, just Mac. Someone has to know where to find me if we spring a leak."

He placed his jacket round the back of a chair, loosened his tie and pushed up his shirt sleeves.

She watched him broodingly. "Don't make yourself too comfortable. You're not staying."

"Relax. We're nearing the end of the cruise. I just wanted to spend a little time with you. Where's the harm in that?"

He turned his attention to a bottle of Champagne and a couple of glasses standing on the table and Kate surmised he had brought them with him. As he pulled the cork and filled the glasses, an involuntary sigh escaped her lips.

Her head was telling her to run into the bedroom and bolt the door but her heart was putting up a good argument for staying where she was. Her heart won and she took the glass he proffered. "Just the one glass, then you must go."

As she sipped the sparkling wine she studied him over the rim of her glass and their eyes met in a blistering exchange.

He held her gaze until she grew dizzy from the impact.

"Now tell me to go away," he challenged her. "I will . . . if that's what you want."

It was no good, she loved him, was almost fainting with longing for him. "It's not what I want."

He replaced both their glasses on the table then took her hands and pulled her inexorably towards him. His eyes had become mesmeric beacons luring her into the dangerous whirlpool depths of his embrace and she succumbed to his arms, her body arching towards him in a purely instinctive reaction.

She was enveloped in the heady ambience of him and her arms crept up to encircle his neck. Upturning her face, she yearned for his kiss, trembling from head to toe in relentless waves of longing.

He kissed her slowly, savouring the moment when their lips met, then claiming her with a provocative urgency that made her senses spin.

"Kate, Kate," he murmured. "What have you done to me?"

She smiled up at him through a veil of lashes.

He put his hand to her hair, tenderly smoothing the waves and touching the soft skin of her brow. "What a crazy hairstyle! It's not long enough to run my fingers through."

She clasped his hand. "Shall I grow it for you?"

"Don't you dare!" His lips brushed

her fingers. "I want you just the way you are."

"Dearest Damon," she sighed. "You say the nicest things."

"Darling Kate." He laid his cheek against their locked hands. "I've never met anyone like you. You take my breath away."

His nearness was like a potent drug on her senses. Every nerve, every cell, every fibre of her being throbbed with desire for him. Was this feeling lust she wondered vaguely? She had always thought that was a male prerogative but now she wasn't so sure. She only knew she had never experienced so acute a longing before.

She kissed his bare forearm. His skin tasted tangy, salty, as if the ocean had seasoned him. Her heart raced at this new dimension of him. Then she saw the anchor tattoo and was at once reminded that he was a seafaring man, a rover, and that they were already into the tenth day of a twelve-day cruise. A shiver passed through her but there was no going back now. She wanted him with a wild fever bordering on madness.

He studied her face intently then as his breath became quick and shallow mingling with hers, he put his hand to the buttons of her pyjama top and began to undo them.

He was taking his time and she grew impatient but at last she was free from the garment and it slid down to make a silky pool about her feet. As he fondled one ripe breast she sighed with ecstacy. His mouth sought the hard nipple and waves of pleasure curled down to the soles of her feet. It was then she felt a throb deep within her loins, a primitive pulse which stabbed at her subconsciousness and sent her spirits soaring to the sky.

He gave a strangled groan and put her away from him while he undressed, tossing his clothes in an untidy heap on the floor.

She took this opportunity to divest herself of her pyjama bottoms. It was as if her body contained a furnace from whence flicker the flames of passion, seeping through her veins like molten wax.

By the time he picked her up and carried her to the bed, her need for him had increased to become a pulsating ache.

"It's been a long time," he murmured, "I hope I remember what to do."

"I expect it's something you never forget," she rejoined, "Like riding a bike." She saw the funny side of that remark and started to laugh.

Then she breathed in his masculine scent and was conscious of his powerful frame. The pillows were snatched from beneath her head and flung to the floor and her name repeated huskily in her ear was the last thing she heard before she was plunged into a turbulent floodtide of rapture where she first floated, then drowned in an undertow of joy.

When her energies were spent he arranged the duvet over them and pulled her against the hard curve of his hip. She realised he meant to stay till morning and was immured in a warm feeling of contentment. Her senses blurred and she drifted into a dream-free sleep.

* * *

Kate woke to observe the grey dawn peeping around the edge of the blinds. She swivelled her head round and as her eyes became accustomed to the shadow light saw Damon sitting against the pillows watching her, his hair dishevelled, blue stubble etching his rugged jaw.

He remained still for long moments, his eyes drinking in the smooth planes of her face then he slid down and planted a swift kiss on her warm lips.

"Good morning, Kate," he whispered. "You were sensational."

She smiled lazily remembering the extent of his ardour and his tenderness towards her. If she never experienced such passion again it would be enough to last her for the rest of her life — and yet never enough! Love-crazed as she was, she had the sense to know she had never been through such an experience before. She really hadn't known what love-making was.

"I love you, Damon," she said breathlessly. "I've never felt like this before, not even with . . . " She gave a little choke. "I want to be with you always." The words of the marriage service were still fresh in her mind from the previous afternoon's ceremony. "From this day forward."

As she gazed into his eyes she saw an unfamiliar look emanate from their green depths, a warmth and strength of purpose — as if her own love were reflected there. Yet not her own!

"Kate, darling I . . . " She knew he was trying to declare his love, for his look was conveying the words his lips seemed unable to utter.

She waited, engulfed in a silence of

expectancy. "I love you," she prompted gently.

The seconds lengthened into minutes and she became aware that his expression was perceptibly changing, as if he fought an inner battle.

He put his hands over his eyes. "Oh God! What have I done?"

He swung his legs onto the floor and reached for his shirt. "Of all the stupid things . . . "

She couldn't begin to understand him and, refusing to be put off, knelt up in the bed to throw her arms about him, pressing her naked body against his back.

He shook her off.

She gazed anxiously at him. "Damon, what is it?"

He reached for his trousers and tugged them on. "What do you want me to say?"

"That you love me."

"You're not serious!" His eyes no longer contained the warm glow of love but were glazed and distant.

A wave of doubt assailed her but her whole being still throbbed from the aftermath of their lovemaking and she reached out to touch his cheek. "Damon!"

He shied away from her.

"Tell me," she persisted.

He directed a cool glance at her for what seemed an interminable time. "Don't put words into my mouth, Kate." The sentence was delivered in an even tone but cut into her like a sharp sword.

An ache churned in her stomach and her breath caught agonizingly in her throat. "But you were about to tell me. I saw it in your eyes."

"No, you were mistaken." He frowned. "Love you? I hardly know you. We're ships that pass."

She went cold. What was he saying?

"I'm sorry, Kate, but I swore I'd never get into this vulnerable position. It's entirely my fault that it happened. You must forgive me."

She reached for her dressing gown

and pulled it on. "I see." Yes she did see. He had strong views on sailors taking on commitments. He had no intention of falling in love. Her shoulders slumped as she accepted the fact.

"For heaven's sake! Don't look at me like that. I feel bad enough about it as it is." A note of uneasiness had crept into his tone — a man being asked to account for himself, on the defensive, blaming her. "Don't take it so seriously." She doubted he was deliberately choosing his words to hurt but they had that effect all the same.

"I see," she said again, pulling the belt of her gown tight.

He picked up his jacket and shrugged it on. "Be reasonable, Kate," he said wretchedly. "You've known all along there's no future with me."

She stared at his strong-boned face, its features unreadable. Was this the same man who had behaved so passionately, so tenderly, a short time before?

She regarded him through a mist of stinging tears.

"I'm sorry, Kate." He adjusted his tie. "From this day forward isn't my scene, I'm afraid. Marriage doesn't figure in my plans."

Her need for self-preservation made her want to retaliate. Summoning her last remnants of pride, she said, "Nor mine!" She backed away from him and continued as casually as she could, "I was carried away in the heat of the moment but if you went down on your bended knee and begged me to marry you, the answer would be no. Why, I wouldn't marry a sailor for a million pounds — and . . . and you least of all."

For a fraction of a second, his gaze faltered. He recovered quickly. "That's all right then, I've had enough aggro this trip without asking for any more."

She was deeply aware of his masculinity — his granite-hard chin, the shiny buttons on his uniform, the spicy scent of his aftershave. He was a mass of conflicting emotions, she decided, saying one thing, acting another.

The door closed behind him and she threw herself onto the couch to sob into the cushions.

Her first reaction was to blame herself for her humiliation. As he had pointed out, she knew his views. He had given her no cause to believe there could be anything permanent about their relationship. She had read too much in his actions. They depicted not the grand passion — Just a busy captain seeking relaxation with a woman. Poor man! No wonder he had fought shy of her declaration of love. No wonder he couldn't get out of the room fast enough!

As she folded the crumpled fancy dress and stuffed it back into its box, she felt the ship give a lurch. She discovered later it was the edge of the the storm that had threatened them in San Salute. For the next couple of hours the vessel tossed

247

through turbulent waters. Kate was slightly seasick, but it was nothing to the greater sickness which lay in her heart.

By mid-morning the waters were calm again and she had the feeling she had weathered her own storm.

It was all past history now, she told herself. She must forget him. She wouldn't be such fool again.

8

KATE donned halter-top and shorts and ordered coffee to be brought to the staterooms. She didn't want to go to the public rooms and risk bumping into Damon. She never wanted to see him again.

"Are you sure this is all you want?" asked Nelson, concerned. "You had no breakfast. The sea's quite calm now and you should get a decent meal down you." He smiled encouragingly. "How about a little scrambled egg? Or some smoked fish? It'll be no trouble."

Kate turned her red-rimmed eyes on him. "My loss of appetite has nothing to do with the weather, Nelson, thank you all the same."

He whistled through his teeth. "Well, I've seen a few broken-hearted ladies in my time, but I never thought you'd be a victim." He leaned towards her solicitously. "Don't let him see he's hurt you, Madam. Put on a brave face and pretend you don't care. Some gentlemen seem to think they can ride roughshod over a woman's feelings."

Kate wondered what he would have said if she told him the man in question was his precious captain.

But his words gave her new purpose. She wouldn't skulk in her cabin and let Damon know she cared. She would go on deck and behave normally.

The sea was unbelievably calm after the night's swell and she leaned her elbows on the rail to gaze at the distant islands as the ship nosed its way northwards through the Bahamas.

She spent the morning by the pool and only saw Damon once when he passed by with the Honourable Esmeralda Fenshawe.

He looked startled to see Kate sitting there so placidly and for a moment his gaze appeared to soften. It might have been a trick of the light, she thought, because he looked quickly away and bent his head towards Esmeralda to hear what she was saying.

Kate gazed after his retreating back. Eleven days ago she hadn't known of his existence. She figured it should take eleven more days to get him out of her system if she really set her mind to it.

She'd been incredibly foolish but, given the chance, her natural good humour would save the day. After all, what had happened? She'd had a short hectic affair with a passing stranger and imagined herself in love. But love didn't happen like that and she should be thankful she'd found out the score before too much damage was done. Okay, she had been hurt, but it was the kind of thing that happened to other people all the time and was nothing to go to pieces over. Tamsin's suffering when Ronnie had jilted her must have been infinitely worse — although to be honest she couldn't imagine anything worse than what she was feeling just then.

After lunch the s.s. Jamestown Pearl anchored off the tiny island of Rum Cay, named after the wreck of a ship loaded with liquor — the entertainments officer informed the passengers gathered by the rail. He added, "The captain has invited some of the local traders to sail over and set out their wares on the deck. This is to compensate you for not being able to go ashore on Cat Island yesterday as planned in the itinerary."

Half an hour later an assortment of traders arrived in a fleet of boats. Kate wandered listlessly about the stalls bearing all manner of commodities such as carved shells, full-scale models of sailing ships, tablecloths, fruit bowls and the usual small souvenirs. But she was not in the mood for buying and the sun was too hot. So she returned to her staterooms to read her Agatha Christie book and at last managed to make sense of the intricate plot.

See! She could banish Damon Penrose from her mind if she tried.

A knock on the door made her jump

and, with her heart beating faster than usual, she called out, "Come in."

"Hi, sweetheart!" Guy looked cool in a fawn open-necked shirt and white jeans.

Kate expelled her pent-up breath. Why had she expected it to be Damon? Hadn't he said "goodbye"? She trembled as she recalled his words. "I've had enough aggro on this trip without asking for any more." Oh yes, he had made it perfectly clear he wanted nothing more to do with her.

"You look rough," remarked Guy bluntly, taking in her bloodshot eyes and taut expression. "I reckon I've come just in time. How about if I arrange a little treat for you? I mean, I don't want to step on Damon's toes."

"There's positively no chance of that, Guy. Come on in. I'm at a loose end and you're a welcome sight."

"Glad to hear it." He bounded forward and put an arm about her. "Well, how would you like to come over to one of the islands with me in the launch? Just the two of us."

"Is that sort of thing allowed?"

"If Damon agrees." Guy rubbed his hands together. "There's this little island, not much more than a rock, uninhabited except for a few thousand birds. We'll be away about two hours, half an hour each way and an hour ashore. Plenty of time to get back before the ship sails."

Kate needed no second bidding. She'd show Damon she wasn't pining.

"Let's go and ask his permission then," said Guy.

She hesitated. "You ask him. I'll wait here."

He took her hand. "You're not scared of him, are you?"

"No." She lifted her chin. "No, I'm not."

Guy led her along the deck to the office where Damon was seated behind his desk scribbling fast in what looked a logbook. He gazed up as they entered and could not hide his surprise at seeing Kate.

"What can I do for you?"

The doctor kept tight hold of Kate's hand as if he expected her to bolt at any moment. "Is it okay if we take the small launch to the bird sanctuary?"

"Why not!" Damon's tone was cool. "It's a romantic place. It should suit you both down to the ground."

"Thanks," said Guy, dragging Kate towards the door.

"Be back by four," snapped Damon, officious suddenly. "We don't want to be stuck here all night."

"Not exactly his favourite person at the moment, are you, Kate?" murmured Guy as the door closed behind them. "What have you done to the poor fella?"

"Go on, blame me," she muttered. "I don't know why everyone assumes it's always the woman's fault."

Guy threw his hands up in surrender. "Okay, okay." He issued instructions to one of the seamen then escorted Kate to the boat deck to watch the launch being winched down to the water.

They descended the steps and got into the small tossing craft. By this time a little knot of people had gathered to watch them set off and Kate felt embarrassed. What must they think was going on?

Guy took the controls and as they skimmed over the turquoise sea Kate allowed the welcome breeze to whip round her face in an exhilarating manner.

The bird sanctuary was just as Guy had described it, a shrub-covered rock rising from the sea, surrounded by silver sand.

A host of terns circled its peak and set up a great sqawking as Guy beached the launch and tied the hawser to a wind-twisted tree.

He helped Kate ashore and placed his arm firmly round her waist. "Got you to myself at last." And he grinned.

She returned the grin easily. She could handle Guy.

They took a winding path round the side of the island and were confronted by a vista of flowering hibiscus.

"How beautiful!" murmured Kate.

"Paradise!" agreed Guy strengthening his grip on her waist. "Shall we build a hut and make our own Garden of Eden? We have all the ingredients for a perfect civilisation. A man and a woman. A doctor and a homemaker. I'll deliver the babies and you can see to the cooking."

"That sounds like I'll be doing all the work," she protested.

He stopped and cupped her face in his hands. As his mouth moved towards hers she turned her head slightly to avoid his kiss, but he had calculated for this and his lips found their mark.

"It could never be paradise," he observed dryly, releasing her. "Because I'm the wrong man."

She lowered her gaze. "I'm sorry, Guy. I think you're awfully sweet."

He turned down the corners of his mouth. "Too sweet!" He caught her wrist in a lazy hold and started forward again. "But there, you'd never have agreed to accompany me here if you'd thought otherwise."

As they approached a grassy promontory they were dived on by angry wheeling frigate birds. Kate freed her wrist and ran. "I don't think the birds would let us build a hut here," she remarked. "They're very jealous of their domain." She turned to gaze out to sea. The s.s. Jamestown Pearl could be seen far away, a graceful sight as it floated among the green islands.

She heard Guy walking over the stones behind her and a moment later felt his hands slide round her waist. "Kate!" he mumbled, his lips against her neck, "You are very desirable."

She gave a cry of dismay and tried to dislodge his hands but he held on.

"Hm! You taste good," he whispered moving his lips to nibble her ear.

She twisted round to face him. "Guy, stop it!"

His cool hazel eyes surveyed her from beneath heavy lids. "I'm crazy about you, sweetheart."

She pushed against his chest. Whatever had made her imagine she could handle Guy?

"Come on, sweetheart," he breathed. "Wouldn't you like to make Damon jealous?"

"No I wouldn't," she declared hotly. "If you brought me here for that purpose I'm afraid you're wasting your time."

"Kate," he pleaded. "How can you be so cruel?"

"Cruel?" she echoed. "I've given you no cause to think I have any feelings for you other than friendship."

"Friendship!" he scoffed. "You can't be serious."

She raised her foot and kicked him hard on the shin. He was so surprised he let her go and reeled back.

He appeared to get the message and shrugged easily. "Don't let's fight, Kate. I've known I was on a losing streak from the moment I set eyes on you." He stuck his hands in his pockets. "Correction, from the moment you set eyes on Damon."

"Oh, shut up, you fool!" She could laugh now that she saw he had given up all thoughts of seducing her. She felt a spot of rain on her face and looked skywards to where a large black cloud threatened the sun. "Oh no!" she sighed. "Why didn't I think to bring my mac? It said in the brochure that we must never travel far without one."

"Tropical rainstorms often blow up quite suddenly," said Guy. "But they don't last long." He seized her hand and they raced back the way they had come. "There might be a tarpaulin in the boat," he yelled.

But they were out of luck. The craft offered no such comfort and was useless as a shelter for it was open to the elements.

It began to rain quite heavily and Guy said, "There are some caves further along the beach in the other direction. Let's take cover!"

"Shouldn't we be getting back?" asked Kate.

"Not in this! We'll be drenched in the open boat. Don't worry, Damon won't leave without you even though he does appear to be rather mad with you at the moment." He laughed. "And he certainly wouldn't leave without the launch!"

They sped over the sand and crawled into the first cave they reached. It was hardly a cave, thought Kate, little more than an indent in the rockface.

Guy cradled Kate in his arms as they huddled together. "What a pity you love our intrepid captain instead of me."

"I don't love him! I think perhaps I . . . hate him!"

"Two sides of the same coin."

She trembled at his perception. "I don't know how it happened. I've never had much time for dominant men like him."

"Ah, you've seen him at work. There's a lot of responsibility being a captain. There are a thousand and one things that come up which passengers don't generally get to hear about — accidents, illnesses, people getting left behind, people dying, disputes among crew, strikes at ports of call, fights, trouble in the engine room, bad weather and rescue missions. You name it — the buck stops at his door. Add to that the aggravation of the blockade and you can see he's got to be dominant." Guy's expression softened. "But you must know he can be tender too. Or you'd never have fallen for him."

She gave a little choke.

"Want to get it off your chest, sweetheart?" Guy invited. "I've taken the Hippocratic oath and I shall treat it with professional confidence."

"Oh doctor," she mocked him. "I'm so mixed up I don't know what's the matter with me."

He took her wrist and felt for the pulse. "What are your symptoms?"

She gave a heart-felt sigh. "Loss of appetite. I'm sleeping badly, or rather, I'm not sleeping at all. The future looks bleak without him, but there can be no future with him." Her voice hardened. "Anyway, he's not interested in me anymore."

"I wouldn't be too sure of that!" interrupted Guy. "But go on. Do you ache at the sight of him? Do you burn up inside when you see him talking to another woman? Do your pulses race twenty to the dozen when he looks your way?"

She nodded. "All of those."

Guy clicked his tongue noisily. "Oh dear, an advanced case. I prescribe . . ." He tickled her ear. " . . . another man!"

She forced a laugh. "What a surprise!"

Guy said broodingly, "Damon and I don't reckon to be rivals for the same woman. I can't understand how he got mixed up with you, but you seem to have got right under his skin."

"You're mistaken. He prefers almost anyone's company to mine," Kate said wistfully.

"Don't you believe it." Guy sounded very sure.

The rain stopped as suddenly as it had started and a magnificent rainbow spanned the bright blue heavens. Guy glanced at his chronometer. "Oh-oh."

"Are we late?"

"We will be. Just a few minutes. Don't worry."

They raced back along the beach towards the launch.

As the craft carried them over the water, Guy shielded his eyes and pointed to the ship. It was then Kate noticed the flicker of a signalling lamp.

"What does it mean?" she asked. "What's the message?"

"It means Damon's getting impatient with us." Guy laughed. "And as for the message, I'd rather not repeat it if you don't mind."

Several passengers lined the decks to watch them arrive and they were treated to a slow handclap.

"What a fuss!" said Guy. "We're only fifteen minutes late."

They were met by a junior officer

who told them they were requested to report to the captain's office, pronto!

Guy laughed out loud. "Time to face the music, sweetheart."

"Why should I?" asked Kate. "I'm a passenger. He can't reprimand me."

"Might as well do as he says," Guy pointed out. "If you defy him he'll only come to your staterooms and confront you there."

Kate saw the truth in this and followed him meekly to the office where Damon stood in the middle of the floor, his expression as black as that recent thunder cloud.

In the armchair sat the Honourable Esmeralda Fenshawe. She had her back to the door, but must have heard them come in and continued with what she was saying. "Those Ashley women are quite a pair. One lands an officer in the brig for fighting over her and the other holds up the ship while she goes for an afternoon of passion on a desert island."

Kate stared angrily at the back of the

woman's head. Was that what everyone thought? What Damon thought? She supposed it was a reasonable assumption. Guy probably had a reputation for taking women to uninhabited islands. And he had come on rather strong. She couldn't have been the first he had taken to that particular island for he had known about the caves. Kate felt her face flare.

Damon's eyes darted from Kate to Guy and back again, then he glanced down at the redhead, his voice low and ominous. "Would you mind leaving us, my dear?"

"Not at all." She rose gracefully and swept towards the door. "Don't be too hard on them, Damon. It's only human nature after all."

The bitch! thought Kate.

Damon walked to the door and opened it for the woman to pass through, then swung the notice round to read KNOCK AND WAIT and closed the door firmly.

There was a short pause while he

crossed the room to take the phone off the hook, then he turned to face the doctor.

"What the hell do you think you're playing at, Lewis?" he demanded.

"Oh, it's Lewis now, is it?" asked Guy, completely undaunted.

Kate felt weak at the knees and sat down on a hard-backed chair, watching the two men warily.

"The sailing's been delayed for fifteen minutes because of your behaviour." The throb of the engines as the ship got under way cut across Damon's words. "I take it you have a plausible excuse?"

Guy grinned suggestively at Kate. She could have killed him!

"You didn't expect us to return in all that rain, did you?" he asked innocently. "We took shelter — in a cosy cave."

Damon snapped, "Do you realise this ship has been without a doctor all afternoon?"

"Aw, come on!" Guy shrugged

expressively. "You okayed the whole thing and I left my senior nursing officer in charge. That's always been good enough for you before. What are you beefing about? Because the ship's been without a doctor all afternoon and we're fifteen minutes late getting away? The hell you are! The point in question is not that the doctor's been missing, but who else has been missing."

Damon turned his head and his eyes bored into Kate. He was remembering their lovemaking, she thought. Remembering the passion he had aroused in her and wondering if Guy had managed to do the same. Wondering if she had found consolation in the charming doctor's arms.

Guy's expression could only be described as a smirk as he taunted, "The question is, Damon, did they or didn't they?"

Damon's fist shot out and struck Guy squarely on the jaw. The attack was so unexpected that the doctor was

268

caught off guard and went crashing to the floor.

Kate caught her breath in dismay unable to believe the evidence of her eyes.

Guy scrambled to his feet and moved his chin about with his hand as a trickle of blood ran down from his mouth.

"Oh boy! Got it in one, did I?" He grinned and muttered. "Stop all engines! Man overboard!"

Damon flexed his hand menacingly.

Guy hastily took a step backward, feigning fear. "Keep away from me, Damon! If you hit me again, I'll hit you back." He grinned briefly and scoffed, "Where's that unemotional approach, that old *sang-froid* you always employ, for matters concerning women?"

Damon looked stunned as if he'd just woken from sleep-walking. He made a visible effort to control himself. "Forgive me, Guy. I don't know what got into me."

"Don't you?" asked the doctor sarcastically.

"Do you want to report me for that punch?" asked Damon.

"No! I make allowances for love-sick fools."

Kate was puzzled. She was well aware that they were fighting over her, but that didn't make Damon a love-sick fool. It merely strengthened her long-held belief that man regarded women as their personal possessions, even after they had discarded them.

Damon smiled wearily. "Aw, shut up, Guy, and go away, there's a good chap!"

Guy went to the door and yanked it open. "Pull yourself together, Skipper, and don't be a bigger jerk than I took you for."

He went out and Kate rose from her chair to make her escape too.

"May I go now?" It was the first time she had spoken since she entered the room.

"I think you'd better."

Head high, she crossed to the door, but paused on the threshold. "By the

270

way," she said quietly, "They didn't."

Damon, bending over a chart on the desk, gave no indication of having heard.

It was the last night on board and time for the farewell dinner. Kate changed into a long white silk dress with a high neckline and cowl hood which she draped over her head, demure and nunlike. She had run a pale pink lipstick over her mouth and highlighted her eyes with azure shadow and smoky kohl liner to emphasize their blueness, but no amount of make-up could disguise her general air of despondency.

As she crossed the deck towards the restaurant she heard someone call her name.

"Mrs Ashley, isn't it? Kate!"

She paused and studied the handsome athletic-looking young officer addressing her. He seemed vaguely familiar but she couldn't place him. Then he raked his fingers through his bronze quiff of hair she remembered who he was.

"Sparks Ingram!" she declared. "I

thought you were confined to your cabin. What happened?" She forced a grin. "You didn't break out, did you?"

"I was under cabin arrest till half an hour ago, but the old man suddenly decided to let me off the hook." Sparks looked bemused. "He tore me off a strip and said the matter had been dropped. Can't think what's got into him. It's strictly out of character. He must have a touch of the sun."

Kate's senses reeled. There was no denying Damon was a fair man. He couldn't allow Sparks to be punished for using his fists over a woman when he had done the same. Hm! she mused, Tamsin may have been instumental in putting Sparks in the brig but she, Kate, had got him out, belatedly achieving what she'd set out to do a week ago.

"I'm cut up about Tamsin's marriage," Sparks said.

"Oh, it was always on the cards," explained Kate. "You must have known this was supposed to be her honeymoon cruise."

"Yes, but I fell for her in a big way."

Kate was sceptical. "After one day?"

"It can happen like that. A cruise telescopes time." He jutted his jaw. "Dammit! This voyage has been a farce!"

"I'm inclined to agree with you," rejoined Kate bitterly.

He seemed anxious to talk and Kate commiserated with him for a few minutes, after which he escorted her to the dining-room. They were met by a steward who informed Kate she had been selected to sit at the captain's table.

Her mouth dropped open in surprise.

"Well, congratulations to you! You've hit the jackpot!" grinned Sparks facetiously. "How lucky can you get!"

She smiled wanly at him and stared round wildly, wondering if she could change it. But her encounter with the young man had made her late and everyone appeared to be well into the soup course. For a moment she contemplated forgoing the meal altogether, then she recalled Nelson's advice. She wouldn't give Damon that satisfaction.

He watched her approach and stood up, his eyes trailing lazily over the white gown clinging so appealingly to her figure, before holding out the chair on his right. She slid into it acknowledging to herself the tumult in her breast at the proximity of him. As she fumbled awkwardly with her hood, she felt his hands take it and smooth it about her shoulders.

She thanked him, completely un-nerved, and nodded to the other guests.

They introduced themselves and wanted to know who she was.

"Kate Ashley," she said shaking hands with everyone, even Damon. She hadn't meant to but he grabbed her hand and pumped it up and down.

There were eight other table guests, two married couples — one elderly the other about her age — an old distinguished looking man travelling alone and three giggly young women from Edinburgh who seemed to be overcome at being chosen to sit with the captain.

She realised with a start that Damon was holding out the basket of bread rolls to her. She refused politely and stared at his hands, recalling how they had trailed over her body. She remembered the havoc they had caused to her senses. A raw ache gnawed in the pit of her stomach making her catch her breath. Slowly lifting her gaze she saw him studying her in turn, his face an unreadable mask.

She looked at the menu and decided to choose normally although she suspected she was off her food.

As she gave her order to the table steward the conversation centred on the book the elderly man was in the process of writing. He had been an ambassador and had led an exciting life by all accounts.

He engaged Kate in conversation asking if she had enjoyed her cruise. She endeavoured to answer cheerfully.

Damon was listening she could see, despite the fact he was deep in conversation with one of the married couples. "Oh yes," she said extra loudly, "I've had the most wonderful holiday of my life, especially the last few days. They were so fantastic I shall remember them for the rest of my life." She almost carried it off but was chagrined as she ended to hear a little choke in her voice.

One of the married women suggested the captain should write a book and the Scots girls broke out into fresh giggling.

Resolutely Kate took her spoon to the boeuf consomme, only to find she couldn't swallow. Oh God! she thought miserably, the meal was bound to last for an hour. How could she endure his nearness? She was thankful she didn't have to make conversation with him — everyone else was doing that and the laughter flowed freely.

The fish course arrived and Kate picked a few almonds from the top of the trout to eat, before giving up. The dish was cooked to perfection and normally she would have enjoyed it. Why had she insisted on taking her place at the table? Why had she ordered four of the seven courses? It would have done no harm to miss this meal. She'd been eating far too much during the cruise anyway . . .

Damon had just told a joke about three sailors in a bar which Kate hadn't followed too closely. As he reached the punchline his lips smiled crookedly — those lips which had planted scalding kisses across her breasts and sent her to the very edge of desire — and beyond . . .

She managed to eat half of the guinea-fowl, but baulked at the strawberry surprise. Instead she sat there playing with her glass.

Everywhere she looked Damon was in the corner of her vision dominating her consciousness. She could think of nothing but his arms about her, his lips on hers and the thrill that had enveloped her in that rapturous moment when she had thought she saw the lovelight in his eyes. Eleven days to get over him? She doubted if eleven years would do the trick. Even the memory of his betrayal couldn't stop her loving him. She experienced a depressing thought. The future was going to be very bleak indeed. How would she get through the days? She had been looking forward to doing her own thing without her husband Peter breathing down her neck. Now she didn't even want to think about the future.

She jumped as Damon topped up her glass with white wine.

"You're not eating enough to feed a mouse," he observed, addressing her directly for the first time that evening.

She realised with a jolt that he must have been watching her despite his apparent unconcern.

"Is there something wrong? Would you like to re-order?" He stood up. "I'll get the steward."

"No, no, please. I'm not hungry."

He sat down and turned to replace the wine bottle in the ice bucket. She studied his hair, remembering the soft springy feel of it beneath her fingers and the coarser hair on his chest . . . As she choked on her wine, he turned swiftly and thumped her on the back. It was all too much for her, she decided, his sheer animal magnetism was smothering her.

"Excuse me," she murmured, rising. "I need some air."

He stood up and his eyes mellowed. "Are you all right?"

"Perfectly, thank you." She grabbed her clutch-bag and fled.

Outside on the deck, Tamsin and Ronnie were sitting holding hands.

Kate stopped before them and took a steadying breath. She smiled down at them. "I thought you two had hibernated."

Tamsin stretched lazily. "Just catching up on the honeymoon." She gazed adoringly at Ronnie. "It's so wonderful being married."

"And you're an expert," drawled Kate, "having been married all of twenty-four hours."

"Twenty-nine hours," corrected Ronnie, giving his wife a secret smile.

Kate turned away, her eyes misting. She begrudged Tamsin and Ronnie nothing, but their delight in each other served to underline her own unhappiness. What a mess she was, she thought bitterly. Was she ever going to be able to hold her head up again and look the world in the eye?

★ ★ ★

Kate, attired in a bathrobe, her short cap of hair glistening from the shower, was sitting on the couch drinking her early morning tea when she heard the door open and close behind her.

She turned her head and was

surprised to see Damon standing there.

"You have a nerve to come here," she protested placing her cup and saucer on the table and rising to face him.

"I know." He skimmed his cap across the room in the direction of the antlered stand but missed and it fell on the floor. "But I must speak with you."

"What's the matter?" she enquired, "Guilty conscience?"

"Go ahead," he invited standing before her. "Say what you like. I deserve anything you care to throw at me."

She was at a loss for words. Damon in a self-reproachful frame of mind was an unfamiliar animal. She wasn't sure she could handle it. After a long pause she said wearily, "Say what you have to and get it over with."

"I'm sorry, Kate, believe me. I behaved like an insensitive brute. It was unforgivable of me — and yet I beg for your forgiveness." He waited as if expecting her to reply, to agree to

281

it even. When she didn't he said, "You had me all mixed up, you know."

She sighed. "So it's still my fault."

"Listen, Kate, I want to explain." He ran a finger round the inside of his collar. "You are aware I was married once?"

She nodded.

"We were very young. We weren't old enough to know what we were doing." He paused and looked thoughtful. "She wasn't strong and I left her alone far too much." There was a longer pause this time. "They summoned me when she was dying but I arrived too late." His tone was filled with anguish. "The guilt has stayed with me all these years. I didn't want to make another woman go through that."

Kate was silent while she digested this. The explanation went a long way to explain his motives. Finally she said, "I'm sorry."

He nodded his acknowledgment. "Try to understand my predicament. I'd got my future all mapped out and it didn't include women. Then into my life walked an enigma called Kate Ashley." He folded his arms across his chest. "When I kissed you among the ruins of Cozumel I knew I had to beware. I told myself to cool it and keep out of your way."

You too, she thought wryly?

"I shouldn't have invited you to share the watch with me." His eyes narrowed to green slits. "It was a crazy thing to do. But I couldn't resist you." His lips twisted wryly. "And with my usual conceit I thought I could cope. When things started to get complicated I tried to prove you were just another woman. Then it suddenly dawned on me with certain clarity that I'd been waiting for you all my life." He took a step towards her. "I'm trying to tell you I love you."

Kate thought she felt the ship lurch and grabbed the back of a chair for support.

"And," he went on, "despite all my reservations about sailors marrying, I'm asking you to marry me."

She gave a little cry, like that of an animal in distress. Still mentally bruised from his behaviour the other night, she didn't know what to make of this sudden turn of events.

She rallied her defences. She mustn't weaken now. "You must take me for a fool," she said, speaking scathingly to cover her confusion. "Not content with humiliating me, you now want me to marry you and be a lonely little sea-wife, waiting at home while you go off to sea, having adventures and winning medals. Do you want me to give up my checkout job too? I wouldn't put it past you." Her eyes blazed like blue fire at him.

"I don't know anything about a checkout job." He tried to take her in his arms but she backed away out of his reach.

"Kate, I'm serious. I love you."

"I don't believe you. You've played with my emotions from the first day we met," she accused him. "You made love to me then you rejected me!"

"I was suffering from shock." He shook his head as if he still couldn't understand it. "I've never been in love like this before. After our night of passion I desperately wanted to give in to my feelings, but I knew if I did I would be lost." His voice took on a self-deprecating tone. "I was too thick to realise I was already lost. For once in my life I wasn't in control of the situation. So I backed down. I loved you — and hated you, for shattering all my cosy convictions. Kate, I'm so sorry. If I could undo the hurt I've done you believe me I would."

She was shaking all over from his revelations and her breath caught tremulously in her throat.

He took another pace forward so that he was touching her. "If I don't kiss you soon I'll go crazy."

She allowed him to hold her face in his hands and, not knowing what to expect, waited shakily as he brought his mouth to hers. His kiss was so tender it had her toes curling in her mules.

"I've behaved very badly," he murmured. "Please say you forgive me."

"I'll think about it," she murmured.

"I reckon I fell in love with you the moment you came aboard," he continued reflectively. "But I fought it like hell! Self-preservation, you know."

She knew!

"Guy and Mac understood what was happening long before I did." He grinned. "I've been so jealous of Guy. He's a handsome fella and knows his way around. Of course I knew which beach you were going to. Of course I held you back on the round trip bus. When Guy hinted you and he had been intimately engaged on the little island I could have killed him."

"You very nearly did!" She trembled as his thumbs caressed her cheeks. "What kind of woman do you take me for? Nothing happened."

"I know that! Jealousy is another

new experience for me. It completely overruled my better judgement."

His lashes were smudgy from this angle she noted, pleased to find another facet about him.

"Last night I made sure you were on my table, not just because I wanted you near me, but in order to prevent Guy from getting you into his clutches. You looked so pale and unhappy I don't know how I stopped myself from taking you in my arms — in front of everyone! That did it! I couldn't deny my feelings any longer."

His words washed over her in a soothing, comforting way and she idly fingered the buttons on his jacket.

As if sensing her softening mood, he took her wrists in a light but unbreakable grip then dropped into an armchair and pulled her onto his lap. Taking her chin in his hand he kissed her gently, sending her pulses rippling in an all-too-familiar way.

"Not so long ago you said you loved me," he murmured. "Is it still true?"

She tried to turn her head away but his hand continued to hold her chin captive and she was forced to meet his sea-green gaze. "Of course it's still true!"

He released his pent-up breath. "Then you'll marry me?"

She did not reply.

"Please, Kate?" His lips twitched sensuously. "I'm begging."

For the past few moments she had been submerged in a tranquil dream-world, like someone swimming under water. Now she broke the surface of reality. "Oh no," she said so quietly her reply was barely audible. "You don't know what you're asking."

9

"LISTEN Kate, I've got it all worked out," Damon said urgently, brushing aside her protests. "Guy has probably told you I'm in line for the captaincy of a new liner." He shrugged. "Well, he's told you everything else! This is a prestige job, luxury mini-cruises for businessmen, sailing between Dover and Sweden. They'll be able to actually sell their wares, as well as their ideas, on board. There were one or two after it, but well, my handling of the blockade just tipped the scales in my favour and the job's mine if I want it."

"Congratulations!"

"Shut up, Kate and let me finish!" Damon absently stroked her hair. "My new job will mean I shall be sailing nearer to England so I won't be months away at a time. I shall be on leave on

289

a regular basis and home before you know I've gone." His hands sliding up and down her backbone were doing all kinds of things to her resolutions. "Besides wives are welcome on cruises these days."

Kate was visibly shaken by his suggestions and the extent to which he had thought things through. He was certainly doing all he could to accommodate her. She decided to humour him — to go along with this madness for a few moments more, in order to demolish all his arguments fairly.

He watched her closely, a tense expression on his lean face. "What about that fine boy child?"

"What about it?"

"You want to fulfil the prophecy, don't you?"

"I'm too old for child-bearing."

"Nonsense!" He caressed her cheek with the back of his hand, a strangely soothing action. "We can take him on the cruises with us. Think what a wonderful life that will be for a child."

She swallowed convulsively and strove to keep up her end of the discussion. "And what about his education? Do you want to raise a moron?"

"Haven't you heard of private tutors? I was raised at sea myself."

"Oh I see, we're going to live in your staterooms?" she scoffed.

"No, these will be six day cruises," he explained patiently, "Six days on and six days off. We can live in your home-town of Maidstone if you like. That's not too far from Dover. And you can keep your job. Better still, we can buy a house in Dover. As for your job, if you're good at it, and I expect you are, you can get a checkout job anywhere. But I shall want to take you on as many cruises as possible." He grinned as a sudden thought struck him. "You could even work on the checkout in the ship's shop, if you're that keen. We'll keep my house on in Dawlish and make regular visits there. We might even buy a place in San Salute, so we can keep an eye on our investment. They'll need help with their affairs for quite a time yet and who better than us to advise them?"

"Gosh, we're going to be terribly busy."

He ignored her wry tone. "Yes, it'll be a great life! Commuting hither and thither. I can't wait to start. With you beside me, Kate, I can take on the whole wide world."

"I thought you already did."

"You flatter me."

She racked her brains for more ammunition. "Won't you miss all those unattached girls who take cruises for the romance?" she enquired, eyebrows raised. "Won't you be tempted to stray? Or will you carry on discreetly while I'm stashed away in the nursery."

"That was never my scene and I think you know it. What are you doing, trying to wind me up?" He gave her an impatient little shake. "If you marry me, I intend to honour my vows and 'keep myself only unto thee'. I shall expect you to do the same. If you marry me . . . "

"No!" She succeeded in escaping his embrace and jumped from his lap. "Stop it, Damon. This has gone far enough. It's no good, you must see that. The joke's over. We're strangers. We've known each other for twelve days. I knew Peter for three years before we married. Twelve days out of a lifetime. And half of that time we were fighting."

"The other half loving," he pointed out quietly.

She let that go by, but it shook her all the same. "You can't base a marriage on twelve days. I know it happens in books but this is real life. We've had a shipboard romance . . . "

"No we haven't. I've had ship-board romances." He jutted his chin stubbornly. "This isn't one!"

She stared at him desperately. "I know it's a cliche, but isn't this all rather sudden? You're set in your habits. You like a life of adventure. You can't have it both ways."

"I don't see why not." He stretched out his hand for her but she evaded him. "Lots of men do. The majority of the crew are married."

"You said sailors shouldn't marry." She traced the pattern of the carpet with the toe of her sandal. "Why can't you stick to your principles? What about the measles and mortgages?"

He rubbed his hands together with obvious relish. "I'm looking forward to them."

"But . . . what makes you so sure you want to marry me, of all people?" She looked away from the intense gleam in his eyes. "I'm not exactly a dolly bird." She recalled that Tamsin had told her that particular expression was old hat. "I mean, I'm not exactly young."

"If I'd wanted a dolly bird, as you so quaintly put it, I'd have chosen someone long before now."

"But why did you make up your mind so quickly?"

He leaned back in the chair and placed the heel of one foot onto the other knee. "I'm a man of snap decisions. I have to be. Haven't you noticed?"

"I've noticed."

He pushed both hands through his thick hair and linked his fingers behind his head. "I have everything planned for our wedding. Let me tell you about it. I got your personal details from the purser and spent the night radioing various officials in England for permission for us to marry today. It was daytime there. It turned out I needed the signature of a bishop and luckily I know one. I rang him and asked him to get it together for me. He was delighted to do so."

She gaped at him, unable to take in the full implication of his words. "You did what?"

He looked pleased with himself. "An hour ago instructions were cabled to our chaplin — who is a registrar in his own right — to issue the licence." Damon patted his breast pocket. "I have it here. Guy's standing by to rush through the blood tests. As we're in American waters we have to abide by their rules and they demand blood tests."

"You've really taken my breath away," she said weakly. "But I'm afraid it doesn't alter my decision. How could it?"

He sprang from the chair and seized her shoulders in a strong grip. "So tell me. Am I right in thinking you'll just get off the ship this evening and walk out of my life?" His green-eyed stare bored right into her. "Will you, Kate?"

She gulped. "Yes."

"Oh Kate, why are you so stubborn?" He turned away and gazed out of the window at the shimmering water. "This is crazy. I love you. You love me. What can I say to make you see reason?" He swivelled back to her and drew her into his arms. "Darling, will you please reconsider and say yes and I promise you it will be a great life!"

"I . . . can't . . . We're strangrers." She shook her head vehemently. "You can't know anyone in twelve days."

He nuzzled her cheek. "Kate, I adore you." He feathered her brow with a spate of kisses. "I'll love you always." He buried his lips in her damp silvery tendrils. "Kate, I'll never love anyone but you."

His devastating presence was electrifying and the fervour of his declaration shook her to the core. His hand was caressing her body while his mouth showered her face with kisses. "This is what matters, my love," he said urgently. "Us. The way we feel about each other, not the drawbacks of a twelve day courtship. I feel as though I've known you for ever. Let's forget our bad start and begin again."

She leaned feebly against his chest. "Damon . . . please don't . . . I can't think straight."

He put her firmly away from him then bent to retrieve his cap from the floor. "Okay, I'll leave you alone to think it over. I realise I've sprung it on you. You can let me know when you've decided. But we can be married on board ship this afternoon and be on our honeymoon in Miami by this evening. Just think, we could perhaps drive over to the Everglades . . . maybe rent a cabin . . . Or you might have other ideas." He fingered his jaw. "But I favour shutting ourselves away in a little cabin and making love with nature all around."

She closed her eyes remembering his lovemaking, how he had made her feel it was the first time, his gentleness, his great passion and how she had thought he could never get enough of her. And she remembered too the subsequent let-down. She couldn't live on that kind of seesaw. "No," she wailed. "I can't marry you. It's a preposterous idea. It would never work and I don't want to risk it. It's best that we part now, it will be less painful in the long run."

He watched her reflectively. "It's a lonely business commanding a ship. I convinced myself long ago it was my destiny. But I had a dream that one day a woman would walk up that gangplank who was meant for me alone. When it happened my stupid pride almost prevented me from recognising her." He kissed her swiftly. "I can't live without you, Kate. And I don't intend to. If you don't say yes today I'll follow you to England. I mean to marry you — preferably in the chapel this afternoon."

"You're mad!" she whispered.

"Possibly."

She dropped into a chair and sat there, dazed, staring after his retreating back.

* * *

The moment the door closed behind Damon Kate flung herself into the bedroom, her mind a torment of wistfulness and doubt. Wistfulness for what might have been. Doubt about the wisdom of her decision. She dressed in jeans and teeshirt and began feverishly packing. The cabin trunk had gone the day before but there was still the suitcases. It was as if by getting the chore finished she would guarantee their sooner arrival in Miami that evening.

She sank despondently into a chair, haunted by the memory of Damon's rock-hard body, the way his look invoked her to strange yearnings. Every part of her ached from his touch. But was that really love everlasting — strong enough to withstand the traumas of married life? Wasn't it just a physical thing, chemistry pure and simple? The truth of the matter was she did not know enough about him. Certainly not enough to gamble her future on him. The truth was she was scared. She wasn't one for bravado, never having been called upon to do anything more daring than go to the dentist — and even that had terrified her. She conceded she was a mess.

How could she even contemplate marriage to a sailor? They were a different breed entirely, so unlike any of the men she knew.

But all her reservations about being a sailor's wife were secondary. After all, thousands, no millions, of women coped. It wasn't Damon the sailor who frightened her, but Damon the man.

Damon, the man!

A knock on the door heralded Tamsin. "Oh, you're packing. How boring! I've left Ronnie to do ours. He said he didn't mind so I took him at his word."

"You've got a good man there," said Kate tightly. "See you hang onto him."

"I intend to." Tamsin detected the underlying discontent in Kate's voice. "What's the matter, dear? You're all on edge. Damon, I suppose. What's he done now? Is he being positively hateful?"

"He asked me to marry him — on board this afternoon."

There was a stunned silence then, "Mum! That's the best news I've heard for a long time."

"I turned him down."

Tamsin stared disbelievingly. "You didn't! But why? I know you love him." She placed an arm about her mother's trembling shoulders. "He's a wonderful man. You'll be the envy of all the women in Maidstone. He's so brave and so dishy."

"Oh yes, he's dishy," muttered Kate, "but I don't think dishy is a good enough qualification for a life-long commitment."

"Why so bitter?" asked Tamsin, going to perch on the edge of the bed. "You're being too hasty. Won't you reconsider?"

"For Pete's sake!" cried Kate. "Damon said he disapproves of sailors marrying. He's done a complete about-turn in a matter of days. We're practically strangers. We know nothing about each other. We met twelve days ago. It's too sudden."

"It's long enough for you to know you'll love him for ever, isn't it?"

"Ye — es," Kate faltered.

"Then why can't you give *him* the credit for knowing his own mind?" Tamsin reasoned. "He's not a child. He's a deep-thinking man. Life with him will be exciting. He's so right for you."

"Right for me!" echoed Kate. She tried to close the lid of one of her cases, but failed and turned to sit on it. "We're total opposites."

"That's ideal," declared Tamsin. She helped Kate lock the case. "You'll be able to knock the rough corners off each other. Think of all the stimulating arguments you'll have." Her tone softened. "What's the problem? You're not worried about his going to sea, are you? Being alone?"

"It wouldn't be for long stints. He's going to work near England."

"That's great!" Tamsin's blue eyes

sparkled. "It alters everything. What's stopping you saying yes?"

Kate swallowed a lump which threatened to choke her.

"Mum!" Tamsin's voice dropped a sympathetic semi-tone. "You fool!"

Another knock came on the door and Tamsin opened it. It was Mac with a small gift-wrapped package.

"Special delivery, Madam," he said, sober-faced, placing it in Kate's hands. "From Captain Penrose."

Kate thanked him and he departed. Tamsin watched eagerly as Kate undid the silver ribbon and spread the stiff paper to reveal a bottle of *Joy* perfume.

"Wow! This is the real thing." Tamsin handled the bottle reverently. "Damon's another man who does things in style. It's the most expensive perfume in the world. Even at staff prices it must have set him back a few quid. What a superbly sexist method of persuasion!"

"Huh! He can't buy me with expensive

presents," snorted Kate.

"He's telling you he loves you."

Kate dissolved into tears.

"You are an idiot," said Tamsin gently. "I can't believe you're my mother. I feel so much more sensible than you at this moment. Damon is right for you. You need a strong man. It's the reason you didn't fall for an easy-going type like Guy. Tell Damon yes and stop being so silly."

"I've already told him no," said Kate firmly.

"I'm sure you'll find a way of showing him you've changed your mind." Tamsin grinned. "I told you we'd both leave the ship married."

"I see, so I've got to accept his proposal to make your prediction come true? What with you and the old crone in Cozumel I haven't a thought to call my own."

"Listen to your heart, dear. You know you love him. Marry him!"

* * *

During the morning a helicopter hovered over the ship to lower a television crew who wanted to film an interview with Damon. Kate went on deck to watch the proceedings. She was too far away to hear what Damon was saying but he made an animated speech and appeared to be taking everything in his stride as usual.

Later Kate was approached by Mr Young who was collecting signatures on a letter of thanks to the captain for getting them safely out of the blockade.

"We're giving him a present too," said Mrs Young, "if you'd like to chip in. A small donation from everyone should raise a tidy sum."

Kate signed gladly and reached for her purse.

She returned to the stateroom to find a shifty-looking Nelson replenishing her bottled water. For some reason the man seemed unable to look her straight in the eye and was obviously having difficulty suppressing a laugh.

Puzzled, she handed him a prepared envelope into which she had put the recommended tip plus a bit extra. "You've been very kind to me. In fact you've spoiled me rotten. That's to show my gratitude."

"Thank you, Madam." He saluted her. "It's been a pleasure." His laughter erupted and he made a hasty retreat out of the door.

Whatever was the matter with him? wondered Kate, looking around the room in search of a clue. Finding none she shrugged and went into the bathroom.

She gasped at the sight that met her eyes. The tub was full and floating on the water in an exotic mass were orchids all the colours of the rainbow. There must have been a hundred of them. Stuck in the soap dish was a note held in place with a cocktail stick. The message said simply PLEASE!

Kate perched on the edge of the tub and trailed her fingers through the blooms. Their delicate perfume was heavenly. Damon must have cleared out the shop on board. How extravagant, even at staff prices! Now she understood Nelson's amusement and guessed he must have been involved in the conspiracy, probably keeping watch and letting the captain know when she left the cabin.

As she idled there a picture came into her head of the old crone in Cozumel telling her that when a man gives a woman flowers it means he is waiting for an answer to his question. The old woman also told her what to do if the answer was yes — give him a single buttonhole.

At one-thirty Kate joined the other passengers in the Mainbrace lounge for the presentation to the captain. She noticed the hero of San Salute didn't handle this situation as well as he had handled the television interview. In fact he was quite overcome with emotion as he thanked them all.

"I had no idea . . . I don't know what to say . . . ladies and gentlemen, you've succeeded in doing something that's rarely been achieved before. You've rendered me speechless."

Gusts of laughter and catcalls greeted this.

Kate eyed the half-dozen boxes of various shapes and sizes. "What did we give him?" she asked Mrs Young.

"A splendid fishing rod, dear, and all the tackle. We asked his steward's advice."

"Oh good," said Kate, "He's a keen angler."

Her casual remark struck her like a thunderbolt. She hadn't been honest with herself when she had said she knew precious little about him. She knew a great deal. The sports he liked . . . his taste in music and books . . . his compassion . . . his affection for his mother . . . his sense of fair play . . . his guilt . . . his courage . . . his gentleness . . . It was a formidable list and the knowledge thrilled her.

As she walked back along the deck, her mind wrestling with these new thoughts, she bumped into Mac. The grinning Scotsman thrust a small package at her and said, "For you, Madam. The captain appears to be having a brainstorm. I've never known him behave like this before."

The swiftly-ripped off wrappers revealed an exquisite blue and white china egg with a delicate tracery of thin golden filigree. There was a tiny lock and key and Kate turned it to discover the distinctive silver Penrose medal — Damon's most treasured possession. As she weighed it in her hand she saw the inscription blur through her sudden tears.

She went to her rooms and sank down on the bed, surrendering to the inevitable with a deep sigh. She had imagined she had finished with love but she remembered reading somewhere that if you are finished with love you are finished with life. And now the touch of a stranger had turned her life upside down. She'd tried to act sensibly but it was no good fighting her emotions. There was a limit to the lengths she could go in deceiving herself. In her secret innermost heart she'd known all along that she couldn't live without Damon. From that first moment as she had come aboard, when their eyes had met and his had had such an emotive effect on her, she had been his, body and soul. Why she had to make this circuitous course only to land back where she had started goodness only knew.

Damon the man!

She said it aloud and liked the sound of it.

Pictures of their future flitted like bright butterflies through her mind — living together, laughing together, loving together.

The crone's voice intruded again. A single bloom if the answer is yes. What a pity her dahlias had died. But wait — she had plenty of flowers — a hundred of them at least.

With a light step she went into the bathroom and hooked out one perfect golden orchid. She shook the water from its petals and searched through her bag till she found a pin.

Next she went to the wardrobe to select something special to wear for this historic occasion. In the end she dressed in the lilac suit that Damon had once said he liked. She sprayed herself generously with the *Joy* perfume then went out and along the deck.

Damon wasn't in his office but a seaman informed her she would find him on the bridge. She was aware that passengers were only allowed there by invitation but slipped through the gate marked CREW ONLY, mounted the steep staircase and pushed open the door.

He stood by the open window training a pair of binoculars on a passing ship and turned his head as she entered, as did the seamen on duty. His look of surprise was comical to see.

Damon's frank appraisal as she crossed the floor told her she had dressed perfectly. She declined to explain herself but stopped before him, took the orchid from behind her back and proceeded to poke the stem through his lapel and secure it with the pin.

He stared at her in amazement and she heard the seamen titter.

Somehow she managed to keep a straight face. She treated Damon to a bold shimmering glance and turned towards the door again, the heels of her Scholl mules clicking briskly over the metal floor.

With her hand on the latch she stopped and glanced over her shoulder to witness the effect of her actions. He was staring down at the orchid with a bemused look on his face. His eyes went to her then to the flower again then, as the significance of the single bloom dawned on him, an ecstatic smile spread over his features.

"Kate!" He started forward eagerly.

"Fishing smack on the starboard bow, sir," said the lookout.

Damon was torn between Kate and

the hazard. Duty won. "I'll be in touch," he called.

* * *

"Dearly beloved, we are gathered together here in the sight of God, and in the face of this congregation, to join together this man and this woman in holy matrimony . . . " The chaplain's voice carried over the small group in the little chapel for the private ceremony. The guests consisted of Tamsin and Ronnie, Guy and the Youngs.

Kate's wedding outfit was a cream crystal-pleated blouse with very full sleeves, a caramel silk skirt, a matching gilet and a pair of high-heeled mules she had borrowed from Tamsin. The latter item was going to give her some trouble if she kept them on for long, she thought.

Damon had changed into a black-jacketed dress uniform and transfered the golden orchid to the lapel where it looked out of place. He appeared so attractive that Kate ached just looking at him.

"Wilt thou have this woman to thy wedded wife to live together after God's ordnance in the estate of holy matrimony? Wilt thou love her, comfort her, honour and keep her in sickness and in health and forsaking all others keep thee only unto her so long as ye both shall live?"

The beautiful words of the traditional marriage service rang out and Damon answered in a bold clear voice.

"I will."

Then it was Kate's turn. She wasn't as clear as Damon for she was choked long before she was required to reply. But her tremulous "I will" was nevertheless filled with sincerity.

"With this ring I thee wed, with my body I thee worship and with all my worldly goods I thee endow." Damon had sent someone ashore on the island of Andros to obtain a selection of rings from which he had chosen the antique gold band. She had got word of it and secretly ordered one for him which she now presented to him. He looked pleased.

After the chaplain had pronounced them man and wife they kissed. The first kiss of their marriage was of necessity a quiet experience but the warmth of feeling that went into it bode well for their future displays of love.

They all retired to a small reception room at the side of the chapel where Mac was waiting with a cake and champagne. There were kisses and handshakes all round.

Damon had cabled his mother and stepfather and a lengthy reply was read out by the smiling chaplain.

"So happy, Damon. It's about time you took the plunge again. Thought we were destined to be grandchildrenless. Can't wait to meet our daughter-in-law. Anyone who's mad enough to take you on must be someone special. You're to come to Wales at the earliest opportunity. Love, Mother and Teddy."

"That must have cost a fortune," murmured Damon.

"They sound like fun," said Kate.

Damon gripped his new stepson-in-law's hand. "Much obliged, Ronnie."

Ronnie looked puzzled and Tamsin piped up: "Damon means if you hadn't behaved so badly he and Mum would never have met."

Kate considered that remark and shuddered. It didn't bear thinking about.

"Well, Mrs Penrose?" said Damon presently as the two of them sipped the sparkling wine by the sunny window out of earshot of the others.

"Mrs Penrose." She savoured the sound of it on her lips. Mrs Damon Penrose. Kate Penrose. Captain and Mrs Penrose. Captain and Mrs Penrose proudly announce . . .

He touched the orchid in his lapel. "Hm! A fine boy child."

Kate eyed him mischievously. "What about a fine girl child?"

"I have no objection to that." He

gripped her elbow. "Come on now. Say goodbye to our guests."

"Goodbye? What do you mean?"

"Mac's put a bottle of *Veuve Clicquot* in your bedroom and that's where we're going."

"Oh no!" she gasped. "We can't. What will they think?"

He smiled crookedly. "I guess they'll catch on quickly enough."

She tried to control her trembling lips. "No!"

His eyes glinted. "Only married twenty minutes and already defying your husband?"

"So it took twenty minutes for you to start throwing your weight about," she parried spiritedly. "I don't remember promising to obey."

"It goes without saying — surely."

"Don't you believe it." She squirmed. "It'll be so embarrassing. Can't you wait till we get to Miami? We'll be there in a couple of hours."

"No, I can't wait! It takes time to put the ship to bed. There'll be paperwork

318

to do when we get there and it can take hours. Now stop arguing and do as you're told." He took her glass and placed it on the shelf alongside his own. "Marriage is like a ship," he mused. "It can only have one captain and I intend to be it."

His gentle tone belied the essence of his words and his gaze overflowed with adoration. His expression was telling her that his vow to love and cherish her would be honoured beyond her wildest dreams; that he would never consciously hurt her again. She knew without a shadow of a doubt that in love and mutual respect they were totally compatible.

From this day forward . . . for better or worse . . . till death us do part . . .

"Agreed?" he persisted, lifting a roguish eyebrow.

"Yes, darling," she murmured sweetly, crossing her fingers behind her back and parting her lips for the kiss she knew was only a heartbeat away.

WITH SOMEBODY ELSE
Theresa Charles

Rosamond sets off for Cornwall with Hugo to meet his family, blissfully unaware of the shocks in store for her.

A SUMMER FOR STRANGERS
Claire Hamilton

Because she had lost her job, her flat and she had no money, Tabitha agreed to pose as Adam's future wife although she believed the scheme to be deceitful and cruel.

VILLA OF SINGING WATER
Angela Petron

The disquieting incidents that occurred at the Vatican and the Colosseum did not trouble Jan at first, but then they became increasingly unpleasant and alarming.

DOCTOR NAPIER'S NURSE
Pauline Ash

When cousins Midge and Derry are entered as probationer nurses on the same day but at different hospitals they agree to exchange identities.

A GIRL LIKE JULIE
Louise Ellis

Caroline absolutely adored Hugh Barrington, but then Julie Crane came into their lives. Julie was the kind of girl who attracts men without even trying.

COUNTRY DOCTOR
Paula Lindsay

When Evan Richmond bought a practice in a remote country village he did not realise that a casual encounter would lead to the loss of his heart.

ENCORE
Helga Moray

Craig and Janet realise that their true happiness lies with each other, but it is only under traumatic circumstances that they can be reunited.

NICOLETTE
Ivy Preston

When Grant Alston came back into her life, Nicolette was faced with a dilemma. Should she follow the path of duty or the path of love?

THE GOLDEN PUMA
Margaret Way

Catherine's time was spent looking after her father's Queensland farm. But what life was there without David, who wasn't interested in her?

HOSPITAL BY THE LAKE
Anne Durham

Nurse Marguerite Ingleby was always ready to become personally involved with her patients, to the despair of Brian Field, the Senior Surgical Registrar, who loved her.

VALLEY OF CONFLICT
David Farrell

Isolated in a hostel in the French Alps, Ann Russell sees her fiancé being seduced by a young girl. Then comes the avalanche that imperils their lives.

NURSE'S CHOICE
Peggy Gaddis

A proposal of marriage from the incredibly handsome and wealthy Reagan was enough to upset any girl — and Brooke Martin was no exception.

A DANGEROUS MAN
Anne Goring

Photographer Polly Burton was on safari in Mombasa when she met enigmatic Leon Hammond. But unpredictability was the name of the game where Leon was concerned.

PRECIOUS INHERITANCE
Joan Moules

Karen's new life working for an authoress took her from Sussex to a foreign airstrip and a kidnapping; to a real life adventure as gripping as any in the books she typed.

VISION OF LOVE
Grace Richmond

When Kathy takes over the rundown country kennels she finds Alec Stinton, a local vet, very helpful. But their friendship arouses bitter jealousy and a tragedy seems inevitable.

CRUSADING NURSE
Jane Converse

It was handsome Dr. Corbett who opened Nurse Susan Leighton's eyes and who set her off on a lonely crusade against some powerful enemies and a shattering struggle against the man she loved.

WILD ENCHANTMENT
Christina Green

Rowan's agreeable new boss had a dream of creating a famous perfume using her precious Silverstar, but Rowan's plans were very different.

DESERT ROMANCE
Irene Ord

Sally agrees to take her sister Pam's place as La Chartreuse the dancer, but she finds out there is more to it than dyeing her hair red and looking like her sister.

HEART OF ICE
Marie Sidney

How was January to know that not only would the warmth of the Swiss people thaw out her frozen heart, but that she too would play her part in helping someone to live again?

LUCKY IN LOVE
Margaret Wood

Companion-secretary to wealthy gambler Laura Duxford, who lived in Monaco, seemed to Melanie a fabulous job. Especially as Melanie had already lost her heart to Laura's son, Julian.

NURSE TO PRINCESS JASMINE
Lilian Woodward

Nick's surgeon brother, Tom, performs an operation on an Arabian princess, and she invites Tom, Nick and his fiancé to Omander, where a web of deceit and intrigue closes about them.

THE WAYWARD HEART
Eileen Barry

Disaster-prone Katherine's nickname was "Kate Calamity", but her boss went too far with an outrageous proposal, which because of her latest disaster, she could not refuse.

FOUR WEEKS IN WINTER
Jane Donnelly

Tessa wasn't looking forward to meeting Paul Mellor again — she had made a fool of herself over him once before. But was Orme Jared's solution to her problem likely to be the right one?

SURGERY BY THE SEA
Sheila Douglas

Medical student Meg hadn't really wanted to go and work with a G.P. on the Welsh coast although the job had its compensations. But Owen Roberts was certainly not one of them!

HEAVEN IS HIGH
Anne Hampson

The new heir to the Manor of Marbeck had been found. But it was rather unfortunate that when he arrived unexpectedly he found an uninvited guest, complete with stetson and high boots.

LOVE WILL COME
Sarah Devon

June Baker's boss was not really her idea of her ideal man, but when she went from third typist to boss's secretary overnight she began to change her mind.

ESCAPE TO ROMANCE
Kay Winchester

Oliver and Jean first met on Swale Island. They were both trying to begin their lives afresh, but neither had bargained for complications from the past.

CASTLE IN THE SUN
Cora Mayne

Emma's invalid sister, Kym, needed a warm climate, and Emma jumped at the chance of a job on a Mediterranean island. But Emma soon finds that intrigues and hazards lurk on the sunlit isle.

BEWARE OF LOVE
Kay Winchester

Carol Brampton resumes her nursing career when her family is killed in a car accident. With Dr. Patrick Farrell she begins to pick up the pieces of her life, but is bitterly hurt when insinuations are made about her to Patrick.

DARLING REBEL
Sarah Devon

When Jason Farradale's secretary met with an accident, her glamorous stand-in was quite unable to deal with one problem in particular.